NEIL CAMPBELL is fr collections of short stories, B Hopper, published by Salt, Birds and *Bugsworth Diary*, p Spoons, who have also publishe short fiction chapbook, *Ekphrasis*. Recent stories have appeared in *Unthology 6*, *The Lonely Crowd* and *Best British Short Stories* 2015.

NEIL CAMPBELL

SKY HOOKS

CROMER

PUBLISHED BY SALT PUBLISHING 2016

2 4 6 8 10 9 7 5 3 1

Copyright © Neil Campbell 2016

First published in Great Britain in 2016 by
Salt Publishing Ltd
12 Norwich Road, Cromer, Norfolk NR27 0AX United Kingdom

www.saltpublishing.com

Salt Publishing Limited Reg. No. 5293401

A CIP catalogue record for this book is available from the British Library

ISBN 978 1 78463 037 9 (Paperback edition)
ISBN 978 1 78463 066 9 (Electronic edition)

Typeset in Neacademia by Salt Publishing

Printed and bound in Great Britain by Clays Ltd, St Ives plc

For the Boss

PART ONE

I KNEW FROM the start that the foreman was a twat. One of the first things he said to me was, 'I don't like loners'. Another thing he said was, 'Never give a sucker an even break'. We were never going to get on.

When I was kid I was on the books at City. I'd played for the local team, Audenshaw Rovers, and then I got picked up by Tameside Boys, and on my debut for Tameside Boys I scored four goals. They took me to Platt Lane and I trained there with some of the first team and then I did my fucking knee in. The triumph in my dad's face turned to bitterness and he's been drinking more and more ever since. I played with a lot of lads who didn't make it. You get written off in your early teens. Mate of mine was a keeper at Bolton. He got rave reviews in the youth team, but because he was less than six foot tall at sixteen they let him go. What a joke.

I got some stick in the first few weeks working in the warehouse because though I was fit as a butcher's dog I wasn't used to lifting and carrying things. So I'd sit down on the oily surface of flatbed trucks and it was obvious I'd been sitting down because the oil stained the arse of my jeans. The only good parts of the day were when the birds came out of the office for a smoke. Some of them were well fit. When I was working upstairs you could see out of the windows at the front and into the factory on the other side of the road and there was a fit bird in reception there.

I went out at weekend with my mates Shackie and Scoie. We went to Deansgate and it was always rammed. Scoie worked at Tahiti Aquariums in Ashton and Shacky at Kerry Foods in Hyde. All the lads on Deansgate wore the same kind of shirts. Getting dressed up just made me feel stupid. When I got home pissed I'd sit there on the bog and look at my hands. No matter how hard I scrubbed I couldn't get the oil off them. It was ingrained in the skin on my knuckles and at the sides of my fingers. Even punching shop shutters till my hands bled didn't get rid of the oil.

In a warehouse the way it works is that you spend the morning loading up the wagons, and then when the wagons go out, you spend the rest of the morning putting stock away. In the afternoon you start picking and packing the new orders, and then in the morning you do it all over again. That was pretty much the routine at Manchester Fittings.

At first they started me off in Goods In. They gave me training on the stacker truck and then I was able to take pallets off delivery wagons all day. I'd put the pallets in the loading bay and then use a pump truck to wheel the pallets around the warehouse putting the stock away. Whenever the bell rang on the shutter doors I had to stop what I was doing and go and answer it, and I'd stand there with my finger on the button watching as the shutter door started rising and curling up on itself and the legs of the delivery driver and then the rest of him appeared below it. He'd give me an invoice to sign and tear off my copy and then we'd start unloading the wagon. Sometimes it was just a few boxes, not pallets, and so we'd carry them off and drop them down in the loading bay or put them on a flatbed truck. The drivers always wanted to talk and I'd join in with them. I remembered that one of them was a rugby league linesman. I'd recognised him once on the telly. Another one always used to tell me about his fishing trips to Denmark and how much the beer cost over there. One time the delivery driver was a woman. I couldn't stop staring at her tits and she smiled wryly. I had tits on my mind all the time. I was obsessed with them. The bigger the better.

There was a guy called Rennie who worked in the warehouse and he was a total pisscart. Mad as fuck too. Whenever the Goods In bell rang you could always hear him shriek from wherever he was, 'Who is it? Who is it?' It was a daily feature of the warehouse and it always made me laugh. Rennie had worked there for forty years and the thought of that didn't even make me smile.

The trouble is when you've been out of work for ages they make you take a job you wouldn't normally want to do. After college I never thought of working in a warehouse but they told me I had to go for the interview. The rock and roll was fine apart from the depressing part where you had to go to Fallowfield and sign on once a fortnight. They interrogated you more and more each time and offered you all kinds of crap. But they said the job would be better for my self-esteem and I fell for that bullshit. So I took it and I got stuck there, was too tired to think when I got home, and all I wanted to do at weekend was get absolutely shitfaced.

The worst jobs in the world are the ones that involve manual labour. When you finish work you are well and truly fucked and you can't even think any more. And there's nothing like manual labour to give a man a thirst. If you've never done manual labour you'll never be able to understand that. You start getting thirsty from about three in the afternoon and when you get to the boozer and have that first pint it really is the best moment in your life.

I lived about a ten-minute walk from the warehouse, in a high-rise flat called Lamport Court. It overlooks the Mancunian Way. The only times the traffic went quiet was when they sometimes closed it for maintenance work at week-ends. One night I slept through a fourteen-car pile-up. You don't have trouble sleeping when you work in a warehouse. During the week I used to go to bed before ten just to get the day over with. I was on the seventh floor and it was okay up there. In a high-rise flat the characters get dodgier the lower down the building you are. Don't ever go in someone's flat on the first floor of a high-rise. I rolled home pissed one night and got chatting to a bloke as we put our fobs to the door. In his flat he passed me a can of lager and even though I was pissed I was conscious of the absolute roar of the traffic. It was funny how you could always find someone to drink with. He put the telly on really loud and we sat on a couch that felt damp. The room was lit by a low-wattage light bulb that dangled from a tangle of twisted wires among patches of damp on the ceiling. There were piles of dirty clothes on the floor and a baseball bat resting against the wall. When I went for a piss the water in the bog was black and on my way back I looked into his bedroom and saw a mattress on the floor covered in a scattering of beer cans and bottles. I gulped my can and got the fuck out of there, leaving him slumped in the shifting light of the massive TV. The next time I saw him I hadn't remembered him and the time after that, when I had, he blanked me. Nobody said anything to anyone in the flats. When people got mugged outside you just watched from the windows. The first time I saw a mugging I called the police at Longsight and they never came. So I didn't bother after that. People used to park near the flats and then walk into work, maybe at the universities or in town. I was walking beneath the underpass when I turned and saw a guy in a suit being set upon by two hoodies. He threw punches back but the

4

two of them were too much. They took his phone and he just stood there bloodied and baffled. I had to get to work. What could I have done? That's just the way it was. No sense in getting my own head kicked in. That's why people always kept themselves to themselves in the flats. If you turned a blind eye and didn't get involved you could at least look after your own back. And the higher you went in the high-rise the better off you were when you locked and bolted that heavy door behind you. Nobody was going to rob you on the seventh floor and the views when the sun set were something special, the skies all red and vast and dazzling. I'd sit out there with a beer and watch crows on the roof of the Manchester International College, the evening sun glinting on the glossy black of their feathers as they croaked to each other.

Another night on my way home past what used to be called UMIST I saw one of my neighbours in the flats hassling young girls for money. I was a bit pissed and so I said, 'Stop fucking begging.'

'You fucking what?' he said.

'Stop fucking begging. And your girlfriend's a hooker.' Although this was a statement of fact I'd put it rather crudely and he twatted me in the right eye. I swung back and caught him a glancing blow but then he twatted me in the right eye again. At that point a bouncer came out of the Retro Bar and the scrote that had been punching me ran away. I had a hell of a shiner the next morning and my colleagues in the warehouse seemed to approve. Maybe I was just like them after all.

The lad that had punched me was called Riggers and he found out what flat I was living in. This is why people keep their heads down in flats and don't get involved. He started banging on my door in the middle of the night, and whistling

5

below my window hour after hour, at two, three, and four in the morning. I never saw that it was him but I knew it was. It was a game, maybe something he'd learned in prison, psychological warfare that involved depriving me of sleep. I got out of bed to peer down on the streets to try and see him whistling. I never saw him but I saw a lot of other things, mainly women from the flats getting in and out of different cars and foreign-looking men driving away. And many times people having sex in the cars, the rocking motion and muted fucking sounds.

So many times I'd seen drunken men wobbling home, falling off pavements, stumbling in puddles, righting themselves, travelling by drunken radar and cursing at the street-lights. And these were men I'd seen with suits and briefcases on weekday mornings. I watched the billboards turn over while nobody was watching, the traffic lights changing when there were no cars, the green man leading nothing across the road except an occasional fox that had torn apart rubbish bags and littered the flats around the lobby. But I never saw Riggers, and never heard a whistle or a bang on the door unless it was waking me up, by which time it was too late to see him. Then all of a sudden the whistling just stopped. I guess he'd been banged up for something and was doing a bit of a stretch.

At work they trained me up on the overhead crane so I could load and unload pipes on and off the wagons. It could hold ten tonnes of pipes. The pipes were mild steel and either black or galvanised, in all sizes from an eighth of an inch to six inches in diameter. And they were either plain-ended or screwed and socketed. There was a yellow control box that hung down from the ceiling and it had up and down and forward and back buttons on it, and you put bands around the pipes and then attached them to the hook and then lifted the pipes up and walked with them through the warehouse to the racks. Then you put skids down and lowered the pipes onto them. And when you had unhooked the crane and taken off the bands you pressed the button and took the hook back up to where it rested in the rafters, left the yellow control box dangling and went for the wire cutters. When you cut through the metal straps that held the pipes tightly together they fell apart and crashed against their metal supports sending echoes around the warehouse. It was a dangerous process. If those pipes fell on you they'd kill you without a doubt, and I did this on most days until the lad they'd put in Goods In wasn't getting the stock put away quick enough and I had to go back there.

This lad was called Daniel and later on they gave him the job cutting the pipes. Sometimes customers wanted three-metre lengths not six-metre so he had to cut them in half. This was another dangerous job and I was glad I didn't have to do it any more. You clamped the pipe in a vice and rested it on a rack and you were supposed to oil the blade before every cut and use goggles, but nobody used the goggles because they were covered in shit and left oil on your face and head. You turned the cutter on and the circular steel blade whizzed around, and you adjusted the vice to just above the blade and then you took the handle from under the blade and began to wheel around in a clockwise direction, holding it steady when the blade met the mild steel of the pipes in a flash of sparks. You had to put your shoulder into it and after you'd done about half a dozen your arm felt like a lead weight and there was a silver heap of oily shavings melting on the floor by your feet.

Sometimes if a bloke came in just wanting half a dozen or so pipes in less than a three-inch diameter it was quicker to carry them than use the crane. If the blokes were okay, which most of them were, they'd give you a lift. The pipes were all six metres long so you lifted them up at the end and slid them back until halfway along when you rested the pipe on your shoulder and lifted it. Your shoulder ended up with a black or silver patch depending on whether the pipes were black or galvanised and how many you lifted. And you had to walk carefully with them especially when you turned around because if you smacked some fucker in the chops with the arse-end they'd know about it. You'd carry them to the bloke's flatbed truck and he'd rest the pipes across the roof of the cab and then strap them together and then you'd close the shutter doors behind him when he drove off.

If all the orders were done and the wagons were all loaded and all the stock was put away, then instead of standing around you picked up a sweeping brush and swept all the dust and fag dimps together and shovelled it all into a bin. If one of the directors came out of the office it always seemed to be in a moment when you'd just stopped briefly to have a chat with a driver or something like that, and it looked to them like you were weren't working and that really pissed me off. It wasn't long before I had a real chip on my shoulder about all those fuckers in the office. Just because they wore suits and ties they thought they were better than us. None of them knew I'd turned a job down in there. That was a stupid move on my part. I felt like a mug and a loser and that was the truth of it. When I was in the pub with Rennie after work I drank one pint after another until he had to get his bus. I walked back down Baring Street past the warehouse and over the Medlock and under the Mancunian Way, crossing London Road near a skate park under the overpass and making my way back down Grosvenor Street to the high-rise.

We stocked pipe fittings of all kinds: flanges and valves and couplings, elbows, tees, barrel nipples, hexagon nipples, reducing bush, cross, sockets, unions, plugs and caps, clamps and brackets, Kee Klamps, sockets and hemp. We delivered to places like Boole's Tools in Stockport, and Crane in Northampton and British Steel in Sheffield, and Kellogg's and loads of other places in Trafford Park, and all over the place where building work was going on. But when all the building projects stopped because of the recession we started to struggle. Every month after the sales figures they took us in the office and we had a meeting. And I always resented the fact that month after month they felt the need to tell us we could lose our jobs if we didn't work hard. I didn't give a fuck about losing my job. If I worked hard sometimes it was because that was how I felt like getting through the day. But it was warm in the office and women went past, and we got to sit down, and we kept the foreman talking for as long as we could and the dumb cunt never twigged.

At the end of each day we'd go up to the toilets on the first floor to wash our hands. Each of us would stand at a sink, fill the bowl with hot water and then reach into the bucket of Swarfega and rub the jelly-like substance on our hands before rinsing them. There were scrubbing brushes too, and I'd scrub my hands red raw trying to get the oil and dust and dirt out. But I think the oil sealed the dirt in, and I couldn't lose the shading on my knuckles or the patchwork patterns along the edges of my fingers. They gave us gardening gloves but they were a pain to wear. You had to keep taking them on and off all day to sign paperwork or check invoices or to use your phone and in the end you just couldn't be arsed.

After a while working there it became obvious that a good skive for both warehouse and office staff was going to the bog all the time. Alan called the bogs the piss-stones. There were four cubicles in a row and they were nearly always occupied. You could always hear someone reading a paper. I'd sit there in the mornings with my head leaning on the side of the cubicle, looking at my phone and wishing my life away.

Morning break time was at ten, and we'd sit in a row in a variety of ramshackle chairs. Later I saw a picture of one of them on Google. It was a Brno chair designed by Mies van der Rohe of the Bauhaus design school. An elegant design of tubular steel. The chairs faced the clock on the wall that was above the foreman's desk with all his pigeonholes and the obligatory topless calendar and the telephone that rang on and off all day. The break was only supposed to be for fifteen minutes but if we could keep Alan talking we got to sit down for longer. Rennie said the world record was fifty minutes, or ten to eleven, and that he'd been talking about his daughter's wedding that day. Another good topic was United. But he played along with it sometimes because he wanted a longer break too and when he turned around and looked at the clock, feigning surprise and calling us cheeky bastards, it was all part of the act.

The story with Alan was that he was henpecked at home and that's why he could be such a little Hitler at work sometimes. If you got an order wrong, say put the wrong diameter of pipe on a wagon or bagged up the wrong kind of nipples, he shouted at you in front of everyone. That was his style of management. I already didn't give a fuck and after that treatment I cared even less.

There was a stocktake where we worked a twelve-hour shift from eight in the evening until eight in the morning. It happened to be on my birthday. Obviously I didn't tell anyone.

'Knackered already,' I said to Rennie, as the clock ticked past midnight.

'Knackered? Already?'

'Yeah. Knackered.'

'Another six hours yet, son.'

'Why do they have that massive clock there?'

'So you can see how slow the time passes.'

'It doesn't move, that clock.'

'Don't look at it then.'

'Then I look at my watch.'

'It's double time anyway.'

'I suppose.'

'Got to grab it while you can.'

'Grab what?'

'You're a bright lad, aren't you? What are you doing working here?'

'I could say the same.'

'I'm too old to get a job anywhere else.'

'Give over. How long have you been here?'

'Forty years.'

'Forty years. Jesus. I suppose you're on a good whack by now.'

'That's right. It would cost them too much to get rid of me. That's why I'm not worried when Bourney comes out every month and talks about laying people off. Ignore that bollocks.'

'I work hard anyway.'

'Is that why you've got dirt on your arse?'

'Have I?' I said, getting up and acting surprised. 'I never realised.'

'Yeah, well, you better watch it. It has been noted.'

'It's a joke this place. You work your arse off. And then even if you just stop for a minute someone walks out of the office and it looks like you aren't doing anything. You could have been working for an hour without stopping and then when you do stop one of the people out of the office comes out.'

'Alright, son,' he said, smiling. 'Look, the thing to do is work smart, not hard.'

'What do you mean?'

'Just think about it. There's people here that do fuck all, but they make it look like they're grafters. I'm not naming any names. But watch how people leap into action when someone turns up. The best thing is to always have a sweeping brush in your hand. Soon as anyone turns up you start sweeping the floor. Your trouble is that you're always flying around on them pump trucks. I mean, look at Chris. He never gets off that stacker truck and he's always on his phone. You should be on that stacker, not him. The other day he'd dropped his cigs and he was trying to pick them up on the forks. He never gets off it. Sits on his arse all day and yet everyone thinks he's a grafter. Even that Daniel knows the score.'

'Can you drive the stacker?'

'Course I can drive it. But they've never put me in for the licence. You need a licence these days. Health and Safety. We're supposed to wear hardhats in here, you know, but nobody bothers. And steel toe caps.'

Rennie ate his sandwiches. I finished my coffee and got up.

'Get us one while you're in there. Milk and extra sugar,' he said.

I came back out of the office and passed the coffee to Rennie.

'Cheers, son.'

'How many of them do you have every day?'

'Free, isn't it?'

'But how many do you have?'

'I've never counted.'

'They're okay except for the bit at the bottom.'

'You want to stir it with a pen. Here,' he said, passing me the biro, 'no, not that end.'

'Too fucking dark in here,' I said, stirring my coffee and then passing the pen back to Rennie, before taking a newspaper from off the desk.

'Have you done with that?'

'I've only just picked it up.'

'I'll have it when you've done with it.'

'You're a mithering old sod.'

'Just get it read.'

Rennie sipped his coffee, listening and waiting, occasionally looking across at me as I read through the jobs section in the *Manchester Evening News*.

'Are you reading that cover to cover?'

'I'm looking at the jobs section.'

'Anything good?'

'No.'

'Oh shame. Here you are then. Give us the paper.'

'How can I read it? You keep looking at me the whole time.'

'So have you done then?'

'For fuck's sake. Here. Take the fucking paper.'

'Thanks very much.'

'Mithering old sod.'

'Can you be quiet? I'm trying to read here.'

'Oh right. You've finished your sandwiches, have you? You made enough noise with them.'

Rennie leaned his head away. Turning back around, he held his false teeth out right under my nose.

'Oh for fuck's sake. You dirty old bastard.'

Rennie was laughing his head off and moving the teeth in a biting motion.

'Forty years of drinking coffee out of machines will do that to your gnashers.'

I threw the rest of my cup across the warehouse floor.

'Terrible waste that.'

I sat there trying not to look at the clock. Rennie read the paper.

'How long have you been married, Rennie?'

'Too long.'

'How long?'

'Err . . . well, it was in the 8os, so, a while.'

'Thirty years?'

'Close to that.'

'What's she called?'

'You're a nosy sod, aren't you?'

'Just making conversation.'

'Kath.'

'Kath?'

'Can't you just shut the fuck up for five minutes and stop asking for my life story?'

'Obviously touched a nerve.'

'Look, just give it a rest.'

'What did you have on your sandwiches?'

'Stand at ease.'

'Stand at ease?'

'Cheese.'

'Cheese? Weren't they a bit dry?'

'I like cheese.'

'No worries.'

On the radio, Elvis's version of 'Follow that Dream' came on.

'Turn this up,' said Rennie, before singing along to the first verse.

I turned up the radio.

Chris and Barry came round the corner and sat in the empty chairs.

'Go on, Rennie, lad! Belt it out. He used to be a singer, you know. Club singer.'

Rennie stopped singing.

'What have you stopped for? Beautiful that, Rennie. Now turn that radio down, for fuck's sake. Get us a coffee, Baz, while you're in there. Shithead, you still awake?'

'Just about.'

'Have you cleaned that oil off your arse yet?'

'Very funny.'

'Lazy fucker. Here, Rennie, what's the Bobby Moore? Are we finishing at eight or what?'

'Yes, we always finish at eight, every year. And every year you always ask me when we're going to finish. Where's Alan anyway?'

'Haven't seen him.'

Barry came out with two coffees.

''Ere, Baz, is Alan in there?'

'Of course he is. Sat with Alison, isn't he?'

'Something going on there, Baz.'

'Nah, not Alan.'

'Might be playing away.'

'More chance of him going with one of them pros outside.'

'That's Bourney, isn't it?'

'Probably.'

'Who's Bourney?'

'Fucking hell, you don't know who Bourney is? He's the guy who takes us in the office every month and tells us we are all going on the rock and roll.'

'Oh, right.'

'Anyway, Baz, how's the glass back?'

'Got to be careful. Might happen to you one day. See if you laugh then.'

'Glass back?'

'Yeah, he's got a glass back. That's why he's on the Pat and Mick all the time.'

'All the time? How do you work that one out?'

'Alright, Baz, I'm only having a laugh.'

'You'll see. One day you'll get it. Working here it's only a matter of time.'

'Alright, mate, I'm only pulling your pants down.'

Alan the foreman turned up.

'Hey, hey, hey, what the fucking hell is this? What does that clock say?'

'Alright, Al. Here, when was the last time you went to O.T.?'

'Fuck off. I'm not falling for that one again. Get off your arses.'

We were in another part of the dimly lit warehouse. Freight trains passed through platform 14 at Piccadilly Station. I sat with Rennie on top of wooden storage units, counting fittings into boxes.

'Rennie, do you really count them all?'

'I'm counting. Shut up.'

I counted the fittings into the box, dropping them in one by one. Then I wrote a number on a piece of card and put the label into the box.

'Look, you count the ones with a few in and then when there's loads just make an educated guess,' said Rennie.

'So I've been counting all these thousands of nipples for nothing?'

'Really? Look, nobody is going to check them. But don't say I said.'

I counted more fittings, taking one at a time out of a straw sack and dropping them into the cardboard box . . . eight hundred and twenty-three, eight hundred and twenty-four, eight hundred and twenty-five. Then I wrote the total on a piece of white card again and put the card in the box.

'There must be more to life than this, Rennie. Counting running nipples into boxes.'

'Yeah, course there is. You've got C.T. nipples next.'

'C.T.?'

'Close taper.'

'What's the difference?'

'Who cares? Ours is not to reason why. Ours is to count how many and write it on the bloody card.'

'Double time anyway.'

'Very true, son. I probably pay more in tax than you get paid.'

'Tax. What do we pay tax for? I don't get it. When you get your wages it's never what you thought you'd get.'

'I'd be out on Deansgate tonight if I wasn't doing this.'

'Only once a year, son. You've got to grab the double time.'

'Have you ever been out on Deansgate?'

'I went there years ago. Can't remember getting home. Get yourself a girlfriend, lad.'

'I'm not the settling down type me. I'd rather just have a laugh.'

'So do you chat them up?'

'No, not really. I let my mates do all the talking, and when I can see the girl getting bored I go over there. Always works. Let them do all the talking. Go back to theirs usually. You know, the other week I was in bed with this bird and I saw something moving about under the covers. She had her little baby in the bed! I shit myself.' It was a lie. It had happened to Scoie not me. I was useless with women.

'You enjoy yourself, lad.'

'I will. I could murder a pint now.'

'Yeah, well. Be getting light soon. There's another train going past.'

'Have we got to count all these along here?'

'Yep.'

'I'm not fucking counting all these. I can't be arsed,' I said, and lay back on top of the lockers. Just then Alan came down the aisle.

'Flaming Nora! I'm not paying you fucking double time to sleep, lad.'

'Oh sorry, Al. Thought we were on break time.'

'You've only just had your lunch, you shiftless sod. And you went five minutes over on that. Don't think nobody noticed.'

'We didn't. We got up at four bells.'

'Ah yes, but you are supposed to be ready to work by four, now get your fucking arse in gear. This has got to be all done this weekend. Rennie, you should know better. You better sort this lad out. I think he sits down to piss.'

'He's not used to it, Al, is he?'

'Well, there's plenty more lads out there would bite my hand off for this job. You don't pull your weight you'll be down the road, sunshine. Never give a sucker an even break, that's my motto. And don't keep going up to those piss-stones either.'

'I'm counting now, aren't I?'

'Well, no fucking guesswork. I'll be checking some of these that you've done. And if they're out you'll be hanging by your bollocks, lad,' he said, before going back into the warm office.

'I told you to keep your eye out for him,' said Rennie. 'He'll be grassing you up to Bourney now.'

'Who does he think he's talking to like that?'

'He's the foreman, isn't he? Little Hitler he is.'

'Little turd, more like.'

It was break time again. We sat down in the chairs and were joined by Chris and Barry.

'Hey, Baz, I was off the wardrobe last night. Dangling from the chandeliers.'

'When's the big day, big lad?'

'Not for a while yet, Baz.'

'You getting married then, Chris?' I said.

'Hey, Baz, nothing gets past this lad, does it? Yep, getting married. More or less married now. I live there already. The Pomona in Reddish. She'll get the pub when her old queen retires. I get to drink all night and then it's just up the dancers with her. Happy days. Go to O.T. with her old man and my old fella. We're all reds. Happy days. Yep, drink on a stick my Mrs. Bet you haven't even popped your cherry, have you?'

'Ladies' man, me.'

'Oh aye?'

'Out on Deansgate every week.'

'Have you heard this lad?' he said, looking around at Baz and Rennie, who sat there drinking coffee. 'We used to go out in Ashton. What a dump. Full of fanny though. You ever go out in Ashton, Baz?'

'Ashton on Mersey?'

'Barry, Barry . . . Ashton-under-Lyne.'

'I'm happy with my Sheila.'

'How's your Mrs, Rennie?'

'Alright, I suppose.'

'"Alright, I suppose". Fucking hell, the old romantic over here. Looking forward to payday, Rennie?'

'Oh aye.'

'Every pay day he goes out on the lash. We're lucky to see him the day after, aren't we, Baz?'

'He shouldn't get away with it if you ask me. I have time off with my back and they grill me for it every time.'

'Oh come on, glass back.'

'Not funny, Chris.'

'Yeah, Rennie likes his ale. Where is it you go?'

'Connie Club. Can get a pint in there until four in the morning.'

'We know. You fucking stink of it when you come in. I could get pissed off your breath. They won't let him in the office.'

'Once a month, that's all it is. Not like you, four or five pints every night.'

'Well, it's social for me. For you it's just getting pissed.'

'Yeah, but who drinks more?'

'Yeah, but I never get pissed. That's the difference.'

'That's the problem with drinking in this country. It's alright to drink a bottle of wine every night and go to the pub every night, just so long as you don't get pissed. Bet my liver's in better nick than yours.'

'Yeah, but I don't wake up in some gutter on a Droylsden back street.'

'We're laughing with City there now. Ten minutes on the tram.'

'Yeah, you're right there, Rennie,' I said.

'Oh you're still awake, are you? Thought you'd gone to sleep like you did when you were on the locker,' said Chris.

'We better make a move, lads,' said Baz.

'Don't worry, Baz. Alan's up the dancers with Big Plums.'

'Come on, lads. I can hear the lift coming down,' said Rennie.

We all walked back towards the wooden lockers.

'Rennie, if you had your life over, what would you do different?' I asked him.

'Fucking hell, how long have you got?'

'That bad, eh?'

'Played for City. Nah, I should have done something with computers. So I could have got a job in an office and sat on my arse all day like all them lot in there.'

'I was at City. We don't get any mither out here though, do we? I just wanted a job where I could just keep my head down and work hard.'

'Mug's game. Look, I'm too old. Nobody's going to give me a job at my age.'

'You're only in your fifties, aren't you?'

'Doesn't matter. It's too late for me.'

'So you've given up already?'

'We aren't talking about me. Look, you're obviously a bright lad. You went to college and all that.'

'One fucking A-level. What use is that?'

'Make something of yourself, lad. You don't want to get stuck here.'

'Yeah, but the money you're on. And you don't do fuck all.'

'Cheeky sod. I've put forty years in here, that's why.'

'I was on the dole for six months after college. This was the only job I could get. The thing is, by the time I get home I'm too fucked to do anything except sit in front of the telly.'

'That's it. That's how the government keeps us all quiet. Makes us work all week. Lets us drink ourselves into a coma. At least when we're all fucked and wandering about pissed there's nobody going to bring down the government.'

'They're all the same anyway. Politicians.'

'I agree with you. Liars, all of them. Anyway you better get counting again, I can hear Alan coming.'

There was the sound of more passing trains. Early-morning light shone in through barred windows, illuminating flights of dust and glinting on silver fittings.

'What people don't realise is that the hardest jobs are the worst-paid ones. You want to get a job where you like going there. I mean, if you had a choice now, where would you be, here or at home?'

'Well, yeah, but you don't get paid at home.'

'More to life than money, lad. You don't get this time back.'

'I never got that. Why do we work five days and have two days off? Should be the other way around.'

'Just the way it is.'

After the stocktaking I went home to bed but couldn't sleep in the daylight. I thought of how it was all so much easier when you were a kid. Before you realised you were nothing special. The best moments of my life had always been on holiday. I hadn't been anywhere without my parents and I was too old to go with them now. But I had fond memories of my childhood holidays to Blackpool, and I dreamed about them, wished I could go back in time and just stay there on the beach.

We went every year for a good few years on the trot, catching a bus to Piccadilly and then a train to Blackpool North. The last time we stayed at a hotel called the Sea View, near the South Pier, not far from a public park with pitch and putt and bowling greens and ice-cream. The four of us stayed in a family room and most nights I lay in fear of waking up my dad. Going to the bog was a nightmare, and thinking about it and getting nervous always meant I had to go. I'd climb off the top bunk, down the creaking ladder and go over to the bathroom. I'd turn the handle gently, leave the light off and slowly close the door behind me, my hands all soft on the handle, and then piss onto the porcelain insides of the bowl. I didn't flush, just put the lid down and washed my hands in a trickle of water before going back to bed again.

I always had to go and get a paper for Dad in the mornings. On the first day, before we got to the Sea View, he pointed out the nearest shop. In the morning, after he gave me the money from a pile of change next to the already-full ashtray on his bedside table, I ran downstairs, past the brass gong in reception and out down a couple of stone steps onto the street. Zipping up my jacket I walked up the side street towards the promenade and went and had a look at the sea. On the promenade, next to a blue and white tram stop shelter, an old man stood smoking a cigarette beside a big pile of deck chairs. I turned right and walked further down the promenade. I looked into the distance towards a roller coaster, its empty red seats twisting and turning. The first people of the day were going in through the opened doors of the Sandcastle, an indoor swimming pool with water slides and wave machines.

The newsagent's was on the corner of a side street. I went in and got the *Daily Mirror* for my dad, as well as ten B&H for my mum, and then walked out of the shop. I was back at the hotel before breakfast and sat at the table with my mum and dad, and my brother, six years younger than me. The landlady of the hotel hovered around near the kitchen as a young waitress brought a pot of tea to our table. I could see the girl's bra through her white blouse. I couldn't stop looking at it. After we'd had the bacon and eggs and sausage and toast and tomatoes and fried bread and mushrooms, and finished with marmalade on toast washed down with breakfast orange, we trailed back up to the room. Mum filled a bag with towels and sun cream and Dad put the paper in his back pocket and the windbreaker over his shoulder. I carried a bucket and spade for me and my brother. Dad wouldn't pay to hire deck chairs so he put up the windbreaker and Mum laid out four towels side by side. At first it started to drizzle and we buttoned up our coats and just sat on the towels to stop them blowing away as Dad mentioned how he'd 'saved all year for this'. Then he said, 'You *will* enjoy yourselves,' and the rain held off and the sun fought through the cloud, and that few minutes really was the only time it rained. The beach filled up slowly and surely and people ran back and forth, in and out of the sea that was supposed to be dirty but never did you any harm. The men with the donkeys came and you could hear the donkeys' bells jangle as they took toddlers up and down the beach. Beach balls bounced around and floated in the sea breeze above the sands. You could smell sea salt and salt and vinegar. There was the coconut smell of sun cream, and candy floss and ice-cream, both the old vanilla kind and the Mr Whippy kind, and cigarette smoke and wet sand and chlorine through the air vents of the Sandcastle. You could hear laughter and bickering and children crying. We made sandcastles and buried Dad in sand and had ice-creams, and then Dad bought a cricket set. We walked off to find an empty bit of sand as Mum stayed to put more sun cream on my brother. In the shadow of the South Pier, in front of the promenade wall, I stood with the bat as Dad took a long run up and bowled at me as fast as he could. I played my best until Dad finally bowled a straight one and the little wickets were knocked over. When Dad batted he smacked me to all parts and I chased after it. Once he whacked the ball so far it hit the side of the South Pier.

When Dad was tired he picked up the stumps and we went back to my mum and brother. Mum helped me dry my feet. It felt like she might pull off my toes as she made sure to get the last of the sand from between them. Then we tidied up our stuff, dropped it back at the hotel and went and looked for a place to have lunch. We walked past the souvenir shops of rock and fudge and kiss-me-quick hats and masks. There were shops full of jewellery with chains that made your neck go green. We saw cheap watches and sunglasses, and amusement arcades where the sounds of Formula One cars and automated voices rang out. We passed newspaper and magazine stalls and then hotel after seafront hotel, until, sick of looking at menus on the walls outside of cafés, we eventually went into a chippy just off the front. On the shiny wooden table there were red and brown plastic sauce bottles that farted when you squeezed them. There was salt and vinegar in little glass containers with white plastic tops, and another little bowl with sachets of tartar sauce. We all had fish and chips and Mum made sure there were no bones in our fish, and by the time they'd drank their tea and we'd had our Cokes it was already mid-afternoon.

We walked back along the promenade and then down the Central Pier, past more chip shops and souvenir stalls and a Gypsy Rose Lee fortune-telling booth where you could look in and see her hands on a crystal ball and someone hunch-shouldered opposite. Me and Dad went on the Waltzers and sat waiting with our hands on the barrier over our knees listening to the loud rock music and waiting as young lads pushed and pulled us into place ready to start. We whirled around and around and up and down. I felt sick with the fish and chips but Dad loved it. When we got off I couldn't walk straight and felt as green as the peas I'd had with the fish and chips. My mum and brother seemed to find it funny until Mum stopped laughing and put her arm around me. We got up and walked to the end of the pier where there were paintings of comedians and minor TV stars appearing in pantomime.

The evening meal at the Sea View was at six, so we made our way back there in time to get changed. Dad had a kip, and I tried to copy him, lying on the top bunk. Then the gong went downstairs, and Dad got up and changed. So did I. We went to where we'd sat at breakfast, this time for the evening meal, and we sat through all the formalities again, the quiet manners of all but a Cockney in the corner who seemed to be forever saying, 'A couple of beers and a couple of coffees,' and always called the young girl 'sweetheart'. Again I couldn't stop looking at her bra and her face went red.

There was some form of family entertainment on every night at the hotel, but Dad never liked it. So we went out and walked down the promenade and saw it transformed by night, all the bright lights and shining shop fronts and arcades. That first night we went back to the hotel too early and on our way into the bar had to pass the entertainer who stood in a white suit on a polished wooden floor holding a multi-coloured tickling stick. As we passed he said, 'You're late,' and Dad said, 'No, we're early, you're still on.' Some people in the bar laughed, and the entertainer looked more pissed off than embarrassed. Afterwards, with the entertainer sat there in his white suit, Dad bought him a drink and we watched as he put his tickling stick in his suitcase before wandering from the bar and out through the front door of the hotel.

Sitting there among the red velvet seats, with my Coke on the gold leaf table next to my dad's pint and my mum's half, I ate a packet of cheese and onion crisps. Mum and Dad smoked away, flicking their ash into a Tetley Bitter ashtray. I put the empty crisp packet on the table and Dad picked it up and rolled it and put a knot into it before dropping it into the corner of the ashtray. I could see Mum getting more relaxed after her drink and talking and laughing more with Dad. Then Dad said it was time for bed, even though my brother was still wide awake and drawing something precocious on a scrap of paper.

Mum made me hold my brother's hand as we went upstairs. She put us to bed and then went back down to the bar, closing the door behind her and leaving us in darkness. The only light came in through thin curtains blowing around in the sea breeze. I pushed my knees up beneath the covers to loosen the tight sheets. Because of the warm summer night and all the warmth of my skin from sunburn I couldn't sleep. My brother was already asleep. I thought about the bra for a while and after that the tiredness hit me.

When I woke I realised that it was already Monday and we only had five days left. I got up and dressed as quick as I could.

One of the drivers who worked in the warehouse was called Billy and he had some spare tickets for a gig at the Apollo. We met in the Apsley Cottage for a pint and the woman he had brought with him wore tight jeans and knee-length black boots. She looked about forty but you could tell how beautiful she must once have been. He told me she was single. Standing beside her at the bar I was close enough to see strands of grey in her hair, but I could smell her perfume and it went straight to my pants. Every bloke in the bar left his eyes on her, and she seemed self-conscious rather than big-headed. I liked that and spent what seemed like hours thinking through what I should say to her.

We left the gig during the encores and went back to a pub in Bury where everyone seemed to know Caroline. We played pool and everybody watched her as she bent over the table. They all frowned at me. I felt out of my depth and just got pissed. Billy dropped me off with Caroline at her house on Green Street and she made us both a cup of tea. As we sat drinking it, her on a large white armchair surrounded by her two purring cats and me on the other side of the room at one end of a white settee, I just sat there. We started talking about the cats and I stroked them for what seemed an eternity. Caroline eventually got me a blanket and then went up to bed, leaving me there on the settee. I barely slept all night and because of all the lager I'd had I was farting prodigiously. I opened a kitchen window and wafted the kitchen door and the puzzled cats ran upstairs to Caroline. Finally I fell asleep and I woke in the morning with a boner. When it went down I went upstairs to her bedroom and opened the door and she was lying there on her back looking up at the ceiling. Only the cats turned to look at me. Caroline let out a massive sigh and told me to let myself out.

As I walked the Bury suburbs my head was pounding. Waiting by the bus stop I watched a man with a grey beard cycle down the road carrying bags from Lidl and Farmfoods. When the bus stopped I asked the driver if the bus went to Manchester and he shook his head sadly and told me to cross over. Every woman I saw made me horny. Caroline was the fittest bird I'd ever been close to and I couldn't stop thinking about her knockers. Why didn't I just shag her? She would have been experienced too. She could have taught me so much. I could have seen her for a while and become an expert in bed. I thought I just needed to get my end away and all my problems would be over.

By the time my hangover was gone it was Sunday night. The drinking of the night before now made me feel doubly depressed. The only thing in sight for me was manual labour. On Monday morning I thought Billy might ask me about Caroline and I was all ready to tell him that I'd shagged her. But he just walked straight past me.

One good thing was that Caroline said I seemed too bright

to be working in a warehouse. Nobody except Rennie had ever said that to me before. I asked Billy for her phone number and I called her and she was really nice about it but, no, she didn't think it would be a good idea for us to see each other again.

I thought about what Caroline had said. And what Rennie had said before her. The only way for me to get out of the warehouse was to do my A-levels again. I had a look online and started saving up for evening classes at Tameside College. And then I saw an offer on cheap flights to New York, and because I was looking for adventure and didn't fancy going back to school yet, I spent my money on that instead.

My flight landed at Newark airport in New Jersey. From there I got on a bus to Port Authority and stepped out onto 42nd Street.

Among the crowds I passed the Don't Walk/Walk signs and nearly got run over. I craned my neck like a fool and walked up and down endless streets filled with yellow cabs. I passed Radio City Music Hall, Grand Central Station, the Empire State Building and the Chrysler Building. On Times Square there were shoe shiners and peanut sellers. Steam came out of the subways. I walked for hours before finding the Upper East Side YMCA. In the tiny room, my knee aching, I tried to fall asleep. But it was humid between the skyscrapers, and with the windows open all I could hear was traffic and police sirens.

The next day I went to Central Park. It was a bright morning and I looked across at the Dakota building where John Lennon had been shot. I sat near Stawberry Fields, listening as an old man played a flute.

Then I headed for the subway. There was a man with

no body from the waist-down going up and down the train swinging his torso like a pendulum, a bucket of coins carried in his mouth landing after every swing of the arms.

Getting off the subway I crossed the Brooklyn Bridge. From there I looked back at the Manhattan skyline. I took a photograph for two gorgeous Hispanic girls who laughed at my accent, capturing their smiles and the Statue of Liberty.

The East River was shining. I turned left onto the street and walked back across the Manhattan Bridge to admire the Brooklyn Bridge in all its glory, with its stone towers and suspension wires.

I caught a subway to Battery Park and got on the Staten Island ferry. On Staten Island I waited around for it to get dark and then caught the ferry back to look at the skyline at night. The Empire State Building was red, white and blue.

The next day I went to Greenwich Village. I sat outside a café on the corner of MacDougal and Bleecker streets gulping coffee. Looking around I saw the white-on-green street signs, the yellow-painted traffic lights, the poster-filled lampposts and the iron-wire trash bins. Getting up to look around I saw the Blue Note and the Café Wha? And there was the Bitter End, where Bruce Springsteen had played.

I wandered back to the YMCA, feeling the tremble of the subway beneath my feet. Back in the room I collapsed onto the bed. Then I picked up the guide book and read it with my eyes straining, before falling asleep.

At breakfast there were pensioners running to the pool in rubber bathing caps. Opposite me, a fat man smothered dozens of pancakes in syrup that slithered around his mouth and down his front. I fuelled up on fruit salad, muffins and coffee.

I went for a look at the Chelsea Hotel. It was elegant with its red bricks and black balconies. There were gold-plated plaques on the outside dedicated to James Schuyler, Brendan Behan and Thomas Wolfe, and Dylan Thomas, who 'sailed out' from there to die. And I read in the guide book about Jack Kerouac writing *On the Road* there. After that I went to a tiny cinema in the West Village and watched a French film called *The 400 Blows*. The subtitles were a ball-ache but I saw something of myself in the boy.

In the early evening I went up the Empire State Building and squinted through the sunlight at the views. Others stood looking at plastic replicas of the building, not looking out of the window where the whole world seemed to stretch out.

The next day I went to the Whitney Museum, the Metropolitan Museum of Art and the Museum of Modern Art. At the Whitney there were Edward Hopper paintings in a room of their own. I saw a Rothko in the Met, and a long twisting Pollock, and a Buddhist mural two hundred feet high. There were paintings by Picasso and Cézanne. After that I headed to the subway again. Getting off at Union Square I watched lads in basketball vests doing somersaults and back-flips to a blazing stereo.

I read through *Time Out* and saw so many choices, so many things to do that night, and went off to the New School with famous poets and writers reading for free. Walking back out into the humid night, I sat on a bench in Battery Park and gazed across the Hudson River.

In the morning I went to the Bronx and saw the giant letters of Yankee Stadium, imagining what it might be like to play there. I saw *Budweiser* emblazoned on water tanks and rooftops and lorries.

I walked through Harlem, along Malcolm X Boulevard and Dr Martin Luther King Jr Boulevard towards the Apollo. I went into a soul food diner and had black-eyed peas and potato salad, listening as two old men sitting at the counter spoke about black history. I smiled at a sweet old lady dressed in pink. There was a geezer at the counter with a tweed suit on and a feather in his hat. After that I strolled down the street, past all the bookstalls, walked back over to Marcus Garvey Park, quiet save for schoolchildren on the basketball court, and climbed up the steps of a bell tower and looked across at Spanish Harlem. Finally I headed back uptown to 42nd Street, to walk around Times Square among the camera-clicking crowds and the multicoloured screens.

As I sat in the YMCA I realised while looking at the guidebook that I could easily get a bus from Port Authority to New Jersey. The next morning I did just that and remembered the opening credits of *The Sopranos* as the bus headed through the toll gates on the New Jersey turnpike.

In my excitement I jumped off at the stop before Asbury Park. I had to go quite a way down Ocean Avenue before recognising the area from photographs I'd seen in books and on album covers. Walking down the boardwalk beside the Atlantic Ocean I saw the gutted pier casino, blighted by cracked and filthy panels of glass. Nearby, a solitary man sat in a wheelchair, looking out at the sea. Behind him there was a fortune-teller's booth, a seaside attraction that had featured in Springsteen's '4th of July, Asbury Park (Sandy)'. The white-washed hut bore the legend *Madam Marie* on the side, above a painting of an eyeball and four gold stars.

Further down the boardwalk was the rundown Palace

amusements arcade, from the 'Tunnel of Love' video, advertising *Funhouse* and *Twister* above boarded-up entranceways. At the junction of Kingsley Street and Sunset Avenue, an empty road circuit stretched around silent parkland and a greasy lake: the junction from 'Something in the Night'.

I saw the bars that Springsteen played in as a young man: a place called Seductions, a strip joint clad in pink bricks; the Fast Lane, stuck between a vacant bus depot and an empty theatre; and, last but not least, the Stone Pony. Sitting at the corner of a desolate junction, its white-on-black sign stood out from a stone wall, and a wooden porch stretched out onto the pavement, fifty yards from the ocean.

The front door was locked so I went round to the side, where a woman with tired eyes was dealing with a delivery. When I told her I was a Springsteen fan she smiled and let me in. Inside the unlit bar there was a poster advertising a gig for Bruce Springsteen and the E Street Band at the Odeon, Hammersmith in 1975. The opposite wall was taken up with a mural that said *Welcome to Asbury Park*. Like the cover for Springsteen's first album *Greetings from Asbury Park*, the mural was designed in the style of a postcard from the 1950s. It showed the town in its heyday, with the windows of the pier casino viewed from the inside, and men in hats and women in long dresses looking up through the glass at blue skies.

As my eyes adjusted to the darkness I saw a small stage and jumped up on it to play some air guitar. For a few moments I felt like the man himself, leaping around and strumming guitar riffs to the imaginary crowd with a weightless Fender Telecaster.

Sand scraped across the boardwalk in the wind. As I stared

over the waves towards the end of the pier a middle-aged man in a denim jacket went past, walking a tiny white dog.

'Hi. Do you know anything about Bruce Springsteen? I came from England to visit here,' I said.

'Excuse me?'

'Springsteen, I'm a Springsteen fan.'

'Oh right, Springsteen? Hell, yes. I used to know the guy. You been in the Pony? I used to work bar in there,' he said.

'Really? I'm a big fan.'

'Yeah? That's great. He's well respected around here. He's done a lot for the place. My name is Chuck.'

'Do you live in Asbury Park then?' I asked, as his dog pissed in the sand.

'No, I live in Neptune, a little further down the coast. I'm just getting my exercise. Say, you should go out and see Bruce's house.'

'Yeah, I might. I never thought of that . . . it's in Rumson, isn't it?'

'Yeah, that's right. Aces Avenue. But I doubt you'll see much. It is set way back from the road.'

'Oh, who cares? I'll try it. I'm going to try and find Bruce Springsteen's house. Ha! Fucking hell. Sorry. Hey, can you tell me where the bus station is?'

'Yeah, you just go down to Main Street and take a left. It's just up there.'

'Okay, listen – thanks. It means a lot to me, mate.'

'Yeah, I get you. No problem. Take it easy now.' And with that he turned and paced off down the boardwalk.

Wandering through the empty streets of Asbury Park I passed derelict hotels and gardens with ragged lawns. On Main Street there was bright-yellow bookshop. Inside I searched for some *Greetings from Asbury Park* postcards, but the lady in a long green dress behind the counter said nobody had asked for any of those in years.

Back at the YMCA I wrote a fan letter to Springsteen, and in the morning I was back at Port Authority station buying a ticket to Red Bank, New Jersey.

In Red Bank I waited opposite the Amtrak station. Wires criss-crossed overhead and left shadows like cracks on the pavement. An old woman rose slowly from a bench as the yellow bus came to a stop. I asked the driver if he knew where Aces Avenue was and he said he did, though he looked surprised when I told him Bruce Springsteen lived there. When he dropped me off I stood at the T of the junction, waiting by a road sign that rose from the manicured grass.

A succession of large white houses lined the empty road. Leaves in the tall trees brushed together. In the distance a red dot bounced on the grey crest of a hill – a jogger in a red cap coming closer by the second.

'Do you know where Bruce Springsteen lives?' I said, stopping him.

He looked surprised. 'Pardon me?' he said.

'Do you know where Bruce Springsteen lives? I'm a big fan; I just wanted to see his house.'

'You're English, right?'

'Yeah. Yeah.'

'Well, yeah, we live next door to him actually. You see the hill down there? Well, you go over that then you'll see some traffic lights at the bottom of the road. It is just opposite there.'

'Oh, that's great. Fantastic. Thanks.'

'That's no problem,' he said.

I ran down the road and reached the place where he said the house would be. There was a porter's cabin just inside the iron gates and a driveway leading down to the side of an otherwise hidden house. A black 4×4 was parked in front of a garage and a dog lying on the grass was striped by the shade of tall trees.

'Is this Bruce Springsteen's house? Hello? I'm a Springsteen fan. Hello?' I said, into the mouth of a silver intercom.

'Why?'

'I came from England to see Bruce. Is he in?'

I heard hushed words then a muffled expletive, before a gruff, older voice spoke.

'Sorry, he's not in.'

'But I came from England to see him.'

'I'm sorry but he's not in.'

'Well, can I just leave a letter for him?'

'We can't accept anything.'

'What if I just leave it on here?' I said, looking innocently into the camera.

'Sorry we can't,' he said.

'Why not?'

'Listen, I don't want to have to call the police.'

'Err . . . okay then. That's alright.'

Noticing the dog's ears prick up I realised I was about to invade on the privacy of my hero. I thought of an article I'd read about a young Springsteen jumping over the wall at Graceland to try and see Elvis.

With half an hour to wait for the bus back into Red Bank I sat on a fence opposite Springsteen's house. After a few minutes a police car pulled up in front of me and a young officer stepped out.

'Excuse me, sir. I'm going to have to ask you to leave. We can't have you near these premises. We've had a call from Mr Springsteen's security people.'

'Okay, okay.'

He motioned me into the car and then drove me back to the bus stop. It was getting dark when I saw the blurred headlights of the bus approaching and before I got on I wiped tears from my eyes.

I'd never told anyone at work that I was into Springsteen. The guy was sixty-odd years old and I should have been into something more recent but nobody else's music affected me like his. The only reason I liked the Gaslight Anthem was because the lead singer sounded like Springsteen. Even when I was on my way to train at City I listened to Springsteen's songs on my MP3 player to pump myself up. But I never told any of the lads what I was listening to. Springsteen sang about being glad you're alive. A song from one of his albums was called 'Factory' and it described my life and made me feel less alone. I never told any of the lads I'd been to America either. They would have only tried to reduce it somehow.

Coming back to work after holidays is always a nightmare. That's the price you pay for the illusion of freedom. They had me on picking and packing now. You wandered around with a shopping trolley and a picking note, putting oily fittings into bags, or boxed-up fittings into other boxes. You'd wheel the trolley to the packing desk that rested against the partition separating the warehouse from the trade counter and then you'd seal the bags by twisting wire around the necks or sealing cardboard boxes using a tape gun. Opposite the packing desk there was a series of wooden lockers with numbers on and you put the bags or boxes in them, wrote the locker number on the bottom of the picking note and took it into the office, where you put it in a tray where it was picked up by someone in there and transferred onto an invoice. In that brief moment in the office you could look at the women and get yourself a coffee from the brew machine. When you were working you could while away hours with erotic fantasies about those bloused breasts. I could disappear into my own head like that, preferred it to talking really. I stopped wearing a watch, never looked at the clock or my phone until it was close to break time, and kept all thoughts of time out of my head.

One morning I blamed Chris for a wrong order that had gone out. He disputed it. As usual when there was doubt Alan went into the office to find the picking note. He brought out the crumpled sheet with my signature on it. 'Evidence is there. Black and white. Tried to stitch you up, Chris.'

'Fucking told you it wasn't me,' said Chris, before walking over.

'Sorry, mate,' I said.

He walked closer to me and with a smile, punched me in the stomach. It took my breath away and I felt like folding in half, but I just walked off and tried not to show any pain. They laughed behind me. It wasn't in my nature but I should have fought back like I had with the scrote outside the Retro Bar. If anything happened like that again I had to show the lads that I could stand up for myself. That night at the flat, I did a load of sit-ups to strengthen my stomach muscles and lay back on the lino sweating and exhausted. I noticed all the damp patches on the ceiling, and as I turned to get up there were silverfish on the floor.

Every Christmas we went out to the Bull's Head on London Road and when everyone had had a few drinks most of the men and women started snogging each other. It didn't matter that most of them were married to someone else. I shagged a girl with big gazongas called Claire. I felt great when she said thank you in the morning. The good thing was we were off for Christmas and by the time we were back in work Claire seemed to have forgotten all about it. Maybe I could have tried to make something more out of it but I didn't want a relationship with her. I was terrified of getting a bird pregnant. Rennie had done that at seventeen and said it had ruined his life. He said his life was over from that point. Not long after that Claire got together with the young lad Daniel, and I saw a difference in him, how he got more confident, and how much better looking she seemed to get when she was around him. I felt a bit jealous for a while there until he got her up the duff. When she came in to work pregnant she looked gorgeous though. Her eyes were bright and shining and those gazongas were huge and reappeared for weeks in my morning glories.

Big Plums was quite amiable most of the time. But when there was a line on the trade counter he got wound up. The thing that got him most was when customers rang the bell on the till even when it was obvious people were already waiting. Every time the bell rang and Pete was in the warehouse bagging up orders you could hear him curse against 'dumb fuckers' or 'cunts'. On my first day in the warehouse, after I'd been looking in vain for sky hooks, glass hammers, and spirit level bubbles, Baz and Chris forced me into a chair and used tape guns to fix me into it. Then they carried me out in front of the trade counter queue and all the customers pissed themselves laughing. But Pete was the one who ripped the tape off so I could get out.

After my trip to America I was totally skint so I did a load of overtime to make sure I could pay the rent. One night there was just me in the warehouse and Bourney in the office. I turned the radio off and worked quietly on my own. The only noise came from the shutter doors rippling in the wind at either end of the warehouse. I looked at the rows of chairs where we sat every day on our breaks. My eyes lingered on the Brno chair. I walked through the warehouse and looked at all the pipes sitting in their racks. Sunlight fell in through windows and glimmered on the galvanised steel. The cutter sat motionless above the piles of silver shards. Resting on a pile of the pipes there was the football we'd made from bubble wrap and gaffa tape. I climbed onto the pipes to fetch the ball and then I started kicking it into the massive goals of the shutter doors. I practised the technique I'd been taught at City, keeping my knee over the ball as I struck it, but then I just forgot all that and pretended to be Sergio Agüero and David Silva, and just kicked the ball naturally like I'd always done as a kid. I smashed the bubble wrap ball into the shutters where it crashed, and the crash on the shutters echoed around the silent caverns of the warehouse, until Bourney came out of the office with the heavy bunch of keys and told me it was time to lock up. I thought he'd bollock me for kicking the ball around but he had his mind on other things. As I left the building and walked down Baring Street towards the Mancunian Way on what was a humid evening, a blonde hooker in black boots passed me going the other way. I'd heard all these rumours about Bourney before and I walked back to see for myself as the blonde climbed into the passenger seat of his car. I walked back again, stopped at the bridge just past Kozy Knitwear and looked down at the slow trickle of the Medlock. There was a heron there, stalking slowly through the shallows as the dusk turned the waters slowly black. Suddenly I felt my knee starting to cramp. The pain was almost unbearable as I limped past the FedEx depot.

Hookers were all around the area where I lived, coming in and out of the flats and hanging around on the industrial estate where I worked. I'd walk past them every night on my way home. They would always say the same thing – 'You want any business, love?' – and it always made my cock twitch.

I was pissed when I went with them. Usually it was after I'd had a few pints with Rennie after work. He went for his bus and I walked home through what was effectively a red light district. I didn't want any of them to know where I lived so I let them take me to places they knew. Once it was at the back of what used to be called UMIST, near the loading bay. Once against the sculpture of a Vimto bottle. Once near the FedEx Depot on Baring Street. A couple of times in the old Mayfield Station. Another time on Bury Street, other times under the railway arches below Piccadilly Station and the line going into platform 14, down near the Mayfield Distribution Centre, or further round, on Temperance Street near the Manky Way. I had hookers on Helmet Street and Sparkle Street. I once ended up in Levenshulme on The Street with No Name, another time on a disused bowling green by the back of the old Green End Hotel in Burnage. I had a blow job in the car park at the back of The Sun in September. I never went with the same one twice. I rarely saw the same one twice. And I've got no stories about hookers with hearts of gold. They were all as hard as nails and if I'd done anything dodgy I would have got sprayed with mace or had a battering off one of the pimps that slinked around in big cars with tinted windows. You never saw pimps' faces. The hookers stood there talking into the car windows and then the windows zoomed shut. The last time I tried it with a hooker we were stood on the bridge on Baring Street and I saw the heron in the moonlit waters of the Medlock. The hooker was on her knees between my legs. She wasn't any good at it. I think she was Polish. I wasn't drunk enough. I saw her face in the moonlight. I could have just run away. I could have done anything to her. She hadn't even asked me for the money first and she was probably about seventeen years old. I felt compassion for her and it was sickening to me. I zipped up and walked away without paying. I said to myself that it was the only way she would learn.

I walked back past the warehouse and the Star and Garter and up to the Royal Mail depot on Travis Street. I carried on to Great Ancoats Street where I got on the Ashton Canal towpath. Red-brick walls backed onto the water. There were dull lights in small windows. The sound of a radio drifted across the canal. People were always working in shit jobs, wherever you looked, at all times of the day and night. I carried on up the towpath, moonlight shining on the broken glass around my feet. Across the water there was a yard filled with gas canisters. I ducked under a low bridge and the towpath smelled of piss. Someone had laughably called this area New Islington. It was Ancoats. They called the tram stop New Islington as well. The stop for Miles Platting was called Holt Town. It was Miles Platting. Near New Viaduct Street a gasholder rose high into the air and I thought about climbing one of the ladders to the top. But that was not what

I'd come to do. I followed the towpath around the bend and up past a series of canal locks and sat near a tennis court, looking across the water at the magnificent Etihad Stadium. I thought about playing on the immaculate turf, how passing across that green baize would be so easy. I thought about how incredible it must feel to score a goal in front of fifty thousand people, to have them chanting your name after. To get substituted to a standing ovation after a brilliant seventy minutes because they wanted to keep you fresh for the next game. I hadn't walked far but I had to walk all the way back and my dodgy knee was already hurting. In the dark on the towpath I looked back up at the windows of dull light in among the red bricks of the factories backing onto the canal, and I thought that my life was going to be one of working in dull light, not striding out to be brilliant below the sparkling floodlights before an expectant crowd for whom I could so easily have been a hero. I turned around and looked at the gasholder. I laughed at the prospect of climbing it. I looked at the water. I thought about the innocent face of the young hooker. Further up Great Ancoats Street was the Rochdale Canal. They were always fishing people out of there.

I knew this bloke in Wythenshawe who looked after his parents at home. He had been on City's books as a kid too. His parents were both in their eighties and had dementia and Rob looked after them for years, wiping their arses and cleaning up their sick and picking them up when they fell. The Tories reduced his care allowance when he was getting fuck all in the first place. I hated that Eton mob: Cameron, Osborne, Johnson. The good thing for the Tories was that Rob's parents both died and he couldn't put the claim in at all any more.

It was a Sunday night, always a time of dread, the moment

when your weekend freedom is over and the creeping sadness of Monday morning starts to crawl all over you. I just went to bed and I was sleepwalking until at least Wednesday lunchtime, when the working week finally passed beyond halfway. Working had paid for my trip to America, but what about the rest of the year? Could you live your whole life just for weekends and holidays? Clearly millions of people do and that's why they go ape-shit down Deansgate and bonkers in Magaluf. But I always had an aching sense that there must be more. Until I figured out what that was I decided to save for another holiday. I did as much overtime as was going and when I left to walk home I nearly always saw Bourney meeting up with the blonde hooker. But I wasn't going to spend my money on that any more. I wanted to go somewhere else in the world again. I didn't know why I wanted to go to San Francisco or what I was expecting to find there. I just loved the name of the place. It seemed romantic to me. There was a blues song called 'San Francisco Bay Blues' and I'd always loved that. And the one about wearing flowers in your hair. As with New York I got a cheap flight, bought myself a little guidebook, packed my rucksack and got the train to Manchester Airport. As I waited for the plane I forgot all about the warehouse and felt glad to be alive.

The flight came in over the Silicon Valley. I got on the BART, which took me in to Frisco. I walked to North Beach and booked myself into a little hostel there. I shared a room with young people of many nationalities. They didn't stop talking until about one in the morning and then at three I was woken by the bin men outside.

I had no plans except to walk across the Golden Gate

Bridge. But that first morning it was foggy as fuck so I walked down Columbus to Fisherman's Wharf to look at the sea lions lumped together on Pier 39. The fog across San Francisco Bay was all enveloping and cold and hugged around the Coit Tower and the other tall buildings, rendering everything grey. Both the Golden Gate Bridge and the Oakland Bay Bridge were invisible, the sparkling headlights of cars seeming to fly slowly through the mist. Somewhere out in the bay was Alcatraz, no longer a prison but a powerful thought in my mind after all the films I'd watched set there. And beyond that was Sausalito. I wanted to go to Sausalito just because I loved the name, and beyond that was Marin County.

I reckoned the mist would eventually clear and so I kept walking along the shore of San Francisco Bay and right up and around the hillside on the long approach to the Golden Gate Bridge. I started walking over it, the rumble of traffic alongside me. I saw the signs with numbers on to ring if you were thinking of throwing yourself off. I looked up at the giant red stanchions rising into the mist and walked all the way over into Sausalito. I climbed a hill, higher and higher, and I sat there waiting for the sun and the sun came, started to burn all the fog away and the Golden Gate Bridge rose red from the mists, and I looked down on its dazzling splendour and at the surrounding bay that began to sparkle beneath it, and then the sun shone on Frisco and on all the white buildings and it looked a bit like Italy rising from the water. Suddenly I knew exactly why I'd come to Frisco. It was just to walk over this bridge. It didn't really matter what else I did all week after that, because the sight of Frisco and the Golden Gate Bridge emerging from the mist was a thrill they could never take away.

I walked back down the hill in the sunshine and caught a tourist ferry from Sausalito that took me back to the writhing sea lions on Pier 39. On the way there we skirted through the glistening waters of the bay and past Alcatraz, and you got a sense of the distance anyone escaping would have to swim, and how desperately lonely it must have felt to look from the island and over to Frisco all white and shining and rising up to Russian Hill and Telegraph Hill. I looked over at the Bay Bridge and that was impressive too, even bigger than the Golden Gate but without the romance to it.

I had spent all my money on transport and my accommodation in the hostel and so I didn't really have money to do anything for the next few days except be in San Francisco. That was enough for me. One afternoon I bought a bottle of beer and sat in Golden Gate Park looking at a lake, other days I walked up and down the hills of Haight Ashbury and through the Fillmore District. I liked the sound of the Tenderloin and I wandered through there but it was full of winos and druggies and hookers and I thought, I've not travelled all this way to be back in a place like that.

The vibe of Frisco was different from New York. It was more chilled out, relaxed, quieter, and with the hills and the sparkling bay and the wider spaces. Unlike New York it was a place I thought I could live in. There were a load of streets named after poets. And there were high-rise flats on Russian Hill, but they didn't look over the Mancunian Way, and every afternoon when the fog cleared you would get a view of San Francisco Bay. One night I walked up Russian Hill just to see the Golden Gate Bridge at night. It was worth it. The silhouettes of the towers rose above the moonlit bay and the cars flew across like diamonds.

On my way back to the hostel I walked past Russell Street where the guidebook said the writer Jack Kerouac had lived. I'd seen the film of *On the Road* and had been inspired to read the book. It was one of few novels I'd ever finished. I loved the sense of freedom, how he put you right there, described the people and the places. I loved the fact that there was no plot and only really a couple of characters. And I loved that he was working class, talked about things in an honest way and didn't dress things up in sophistication. I bought myself a copy from upstairs in the rickety old City Lights bookshop and read passages of it in a bar called Tosca's while nursing a Canadian Club whisky. The writing seemed brilliant, especially when they got to the hills of Mexico near the end, and I dreamed one day I'd go there and maybe to Colorado too.

With all the walking I'd done I was exhausted when I got on the plane. I had three seats to myself, drank four beers and then stretched out across the seats to sleep, waking just before the approach to landing in Manchester.

Back in the warehouse I was more depressed than ever. Because it was a job I could do easily I was never stressed, but I was physically knackered. That combination stopped me trying to get out. But it was the original dead-end job. I sat there looking into a bag of greasy barrel nipples, counting one after another as the order stretched out into the hundreds. In my mind I saw the sparkling expanse of San Francisco Bay below the blood-red stanchions of the Golden Gate Bridge. The contrast of the two moments was stark in my mind. I thought about Alcatraz too. I looked at my hands, the in-grained dirt, sealed in by the oil and grease of the fittings I laboured to count every day, the hands that every woman I met could never fail to see. The job seemed more pointless than ever. I just dumped a load of fittings into the bag without counting.

I began making more and more mistakes: picking and packing the wrong fittings, putting stock away in the wrong place, throwing bags in the wrong lockers so they went on the wrong wagons and got delivered to the wrong places. I got more and more bollockings from Alan, and then eventually he sent me in to see Bourney. And Bourney surprised me. He said that I was being put back in Goods In and that if I did well over the next couple of months I would get a pay rise.

The next few months I worked as hard as I could in Goods In, getting all the stock put away quickly and nearly always keeping the loading bay free. Each night before five I swept the loading bay floor and glanced back with pride before leaving for the day. Two months later I went in the office and asked Bourney about the pay rise and he explained patiently to me that although I had done a good job and it had been noticed by many how often the loading bay was clear, the sales figures for the company were down and he couldn't justify giving anyone a pay rise. I was fuming when I came out of the office. I felt like a total mug. I'd worked my bollocks off for nothing. From that moment I decided that I wasn't going to work hard any more and that I was going to have to try harder to find a way out. I had to do something else. But what? I needed more qualifications, but the tuition fees the Tories had brought in made going to university seem out of reach for someone like me. Sometimes I thought there was no way out and that I would be stuck in the warehouse for ever.

Chris knew I'd been trying for a pay rise. And he'd been

having a pop ever since I'd accused him of sending a wrong order out when it had been me. We were sitting in the chairs at break time and he wouldn't stop ribbing me.

'Thought you were getting a pay rise didn't you, shithead?' he said.

'No, why?' I hadn't told anyone about my promised pay rise and wondered how he'd found out. I guess Bourney had told Alan and Alan had told the lads. I suddenly felt cornered, like they were all against me, laughing.

'Shithead.'

'Fuck off, Chris.'

'Shithead.'

'Fuck off.'

'Hey, Alan, I reckon both of us pay more tax each month than he gets wages.'

It was an old joke, but Chris and Alan laughed merrily. I looked at Rennie, but though I liked him he never stood up for me. Like everyone else he looked after his own back. He didn't take sides. And he never rocked the boat.

Chris started singing, 'What a shithead, what a shithead.'

'Chris, just fucking shut up, will you?'

'You're a shithead. You blame other people for your cock-ups and you're just a shithead,' he said, rising from his seat and standing over me. I stood up and he pushed me back down but then something snapped. I grabbed him around the waist and pushed up out of my seat with my legs, knocking him into Alan and then Alan's desk, spilling Alan's coffee and knocking paperwork off the shelves. I kept my head down and kept shoving Chris's back into the desk and he was punching me on the head but I didn't feel it, and I kept ramming him into the desk until Alan and Baz and Rennie and Daniel pulled us apart. I could see the surprise on everyone's face, especially Chris's, who clearly wasn't expecting it. Over the next few days I really watched my back. But nothing came, there were no reprisals. Chris had been embarrassed and he left me alone after that.

On the rare occasions when we got really busy Alan always got an extra lad in from the agency. Mark was one of those lads. The first day he came he had a black eye patch over the right eye. He was about ten years older than me. He was lanky and had long, light-coloured curly hair, blonde but with grey already in it. Every night after work he went into town on his own to go boozing. The second time we got him in from the agency he had a patch over his left eye.

One night we went in the Bull's Head, and then had a few more beers in different pubs around town: one in the Town Hall Tavern, another in Sam's Chop House, one in Mr Thomas's Chop House, one in the Shakespeare. We ended up in the Waldorf. There was a match on the big screens and I settled back to watch it, but Mark just kept talking over the commentary.

'Sport is a waste of time,' he said.

'Don't be daft.'

'It is. Bunch of grown men running around after a ball.'

'Takes a lot of skill.'

'My arse. And the money they are on is a joke.'

'That could have been me.'

'What do you mean?'

'I was with City when I was a kid. But I got injured.'

'Sorry, mate. But probably for the best.'

'How do you work that one out?'

'Look, sport is fucking stupid.'

'I wouldn't mind if I was out there, all those people chanting my name.'

'I can't think of anything worse.'

'What? You must be mad.'

'All that kissing and cuddling after every goal. Rolling around on the floor, diving when someone kicks you. And then you all get in the showers together after.'

Just then someone behind us told him to shut up. They were trying to watch the game. Mark stood up in front of the screen, blocking their view. He was tall, but skinny.

'I am trying to have a conversation!' he shouted. I pulled at his sleeve but he carried on. 'I know you plebs love to ease your pain by watching these pointless games, but we are having a conversation.'

'Sit down, lad,' said an older bloke.

'Fuck off, granddad!'

'Hey, that's my dad!' said someone else.

'Tell him to mind his own fucking business then,' said Mark. Just then City hit the crossbar, and the lad who'd first told Mark to shut up walked right over to him and put his face into his. 'Either sit down, mate, or I'll put you on your arse.'

'You and whose army?'

At this, the lad, who was shorter than Mark but stocky and tattooed and with a crew-cut that contrasted sharply with Mark's floppy blonde curls, shoved him down into his seat. I tried to keep calm, hoping it would blow over, but after the thing with Chris my fists were ready. Thankfully Agüero scored in that moment and City got another couple early in the second half, so everyone was in a better mood.

I tried to get Mark to leave, to go for a pint somewhere else. I should have just gone home, but after a few pints I always just wanted to stay out and keep drinking. I thought only boring people had a couple and went home. But Mark wanted to stay. He kept staring at the crew-cut lad. But the crew-cut lad wasn't pissed off any more and just shook his head and laughed and turned away. Mark went for another couple of pints. He necked his and then suddenly marched over to the crew-cut lad, who had his back towards us. Mark put his hand on his shoulder and the lad swung his fist around and knocked Mark onto his arse. And Mark just lay there. Then he started laughing and that freaked everyone out. He was just lying there on the floor and laughing. The landlord came over to me and told me to get Mark out of there before someone 'wraps a fucking pool cue over his head'.

That night he kipped on my couch and pissed on it. After he'd gone and as I launched my sodden settee off the balcony I realised that he was an alcoholic. I was just someone for him to drink with. After that I never saw him again. He was just one of those people that burns brightly in your life and then disappears.

In summer I went to see Springsteen at the Etihad Stadium, and though it was great and I felt at ease in my own company, I was tired of just seeing great things like New York and Frisco and Asbury Park and Springsteen and having nobody to share it with. I needed a new way forward. Drinking and holidays were just temporary solutions. I thought the thing with Chris had made me feel better about myself, but not long after that I woke up in Bootle Street police station.

There was bile in my throat and puke in the toilet. I was lying there on the blue mat and looking through the frosted window high on the ceiling, thinking about the time I scored six goals in one game for Audenshaw Rovers. Cell doors banged open and closed as I lay squinting into the haze of the morning sun.

The day I scored six was the first time I realised I was better than everyone else on the pitch. It was sodden wet and we were soaked even before we started the game. Dukinfield Tigers had won the league for the previous few years but their best players had got too old for the juniors and we had some great young kids coming through. There were two brothers who started playing for us. They were from Abbey Hey in Gorton and because our manager Norman was from there he knew them and persuaded them to play. And there was Daz, Norman's son, six four at fourteen, good at cricket and golf too. Daz was a great passer of the ball and he set up many of my goals that day. I could take you through them all from memory but I won't. I swung one in with my left foot, got a couple of headers, but the best was a free kick, up and over the wall. We played in full-sized goals and their keeper was tiny so I just kept lobbing and chipping him. I hit the bar a couple of times. Everyone was talking to me after the game that day. People always talked to you when you played well. When you missed a load of chances and you got beat nobody spoke to you at all. Dad was there on the day I scored six. What had happened to the promise of youth? How had I ended up like this? Sport is not pointless. It holds the promise of a dream, and the promise of a dream is something to keep you going.

I didn't even know what Lent was really, but it happened to start the day after I'd spent the night at Bootle Street. So I gave up drinking for Lent. I wasn't so up and down. I felt like I was on an even keel. I had a clear head all the time and told myself I needed to get a grip. It meant I no longer went out with Shackie and Scoie for a beer, and any bloke I'd ever had a beer with soon disappeared off the radar. I missed them but I didn't miss the drinking. I realised I had been spending all my free time drinking with other single men and talking about women.

Because I didn't need a drink, and because I knew I had never needed a drink, I was much more relaxed. Women seemed to like it. I didn't have anything to say and so I listened to them. I had learned at last to just shut the fuck up.

I started going out with the girl on reception, Chloe. Her big tits made me crazy. When she first took them out I gazed in awe. I rumpled them repeatedly, causing her to giggle, and then kissed them before running out of ideas. She was impressed that I was going to night school. But I knew I wasn't in love with her so I ended it and she was upset. And then all the girls in the office were sniffing around me and I slept with a few of them. We were all young, nobody was interested in getting married. One thing I had learned was that you had to go out with a girl and sleep with her before you could decide how you felt. I had fucked up falling for that Caroline but there had been no chemistry between us and it was all a delusion. With certain girls it is how they talk, how their eyes become animated when they smile, how their whole spirit and soul shines up through the skin. Even the anticipation of boobs excited me more than playing with them. Maybe that's life right there.

When Michelle came in the office everyone, men and women, stared at the massive tits straining at her blouse. They were even bigger than Chloe's and Claire's. And she wore these tiny cardigans that fell back from her shoulders and accentuated everything. I knew that getting close to her was all about keeping my eyes on her face, which was very attractive, and complimenting her intelligence. The job on the phones was easy for her and none of the other women liked her. I talked to her whenever I could when she came out for a smoke. She was a sweet girl who was going to get married to a lad she'd gone to school with. We were all invited to the wedding and the do was at Quaffers in Bredbury. A few of us went on to Bredbury Hall. I copped off with a woman who'd just got divorced and we got ourselves a room in the hotel there. She was lost and I took advantage of that.

It came as a great surprise when a cheque came through the post for seven grand. It was an inheritance from my grand-dad. He'd passed away years before but I didn't get what he left me until his second wife died, and she clung on into her nineties. Suddenly it seemed I had more options. Granddad had worked forty years as an insurance agent for a company called ManuLife and before that he'd fought in the war. He was a character with a zest for life. When I became a teenager and shot up quickly he started calling me Lofty. He had glossy silver hair. He taught me how to swim and how to swing a golf club, and he drove a Toyota Celica, and they went on holidays abroad every year and he always seemed to have a suntan and to never put on weight. I wasn't going to waste this man's money.

I finally signed up to retake my A-levels. First time around I'd got a D in English Literature and totally failed Business Studies. I was training at City then and I didn't give a fuck. And I'd dropped out of P.E. in the first year. Instead of playing football and cricket they had us doing all these other stupid things like Modern Dance and lacrosse and trampoline and I couldn't be arsed with all that. Those are just sports for people who can't play football and cricket. I decided to take the A-levels that I had the most chance of passing, and so I did English Literature and English Language.

I could barely keep my eyes open in the evening classes. There were about a dozen of us there and the classroom was really warm and after working in the warehouse all day it was really hard to concentrate. In one of the classes we were talking about one of those boring nineteenth-century novels that goes on for ever and has loads of characters and describes everything in minute detail, and the lecturer said she had read it in a couple of hours. This amazed all of us but she shrugged it off. What I like about books is that everything always stays in the same place and you can find what you are looking for in pages you hold in your own hands. Before the exam we were allowed to make notes and even write in the margins of the books. The exams were held in a gym. Afterwards I worried that I'd tried too hard, written too much.

By the time June came around, I had a place waiting at Manchester Metropolitan University if I got the right grades. I remembered revising all the poetic terms like metaphor and personification and all those things, and using them all in my answers, and I hoped this might see me through the literature one. On the day of the results I went into the college and they gave me my envelope. I went outside with it and sat on a bench near a grassy area in a car park of the college. I opened the A4 envelope with my heart beating fast, and when I read the grades I shouted, 'Yes! Fucking yes!'

Everyone in the warehouse knew I was leaving on the Friday. Nobody had said anything about a leaving do. I guessed we would go to the Bull's Head and get pissed, and then maybe head into town. But that Friday morning I stayed in bed and stared at the clock on my phone. Half an hour after I should have left the flat to go to work I got out of bed and got dressed. I stood out on the balcony and looked across at the jam-packed traffic on the Mancunian Way and decided not to bother going in. Instead I walked down Oxford Road and went into the Ryman stationery shop, where I bought myself an A4 note pad and a pen.

Back at the high-rise I went up to the seventh floor in the lift and wandered the length of the walkway. Before going inside I looked beyond London Road towards the warehouse. I could just about see the roof behind the hotel that used to be the BT building. There were trains coming in and out of Piccadilly Station, and beyond them, the Etihad Stadium. Springsteen said if one dream fails then find another dream. That's good advice, but you can't just forget the first part.

PART TWO

H E WAS NAKED and dead. I looked down and saw him sprawled there. There was a pool of blood around his head. I called Longsight police. Even they would come out for a corpse.

As I waited downstairs I saw that his beard was quite neatly trimmed. He'd shaved the hair off his neck. The contrast of the beard and his pubes was strong against the pale white. His nakedness made it all the more shocking. Why strip naked beforehand? To show you didn't care about anything? In the flats you hardly saw anyone else, but I did remember seeing this man once before. As I was leaving the flats to go to a seminar at the university, he was walking back home. It was early in the morning and there was frost on the ground. He had a blue carrier bag and I could see the cans of lager inside. I also noticed that he was only wearing one shoe. The bare foot was blue. I should have said something to him. But what?

In the afternoon I needed to wash some clothes. I poured the powder into the bath and then ran the hot water. When it was deep enough I left my clothes soaking. Then I let the water out and filled the bath again and left the clothes in there for another hour or so. Finally I let the water out, wringing the clothes and hanging them on an old fashioned hanger that rolled out from above the tub and hooked onto a catch at the other end of the bath.

They started me in the back of the bookshop, unloading wagons and checking off invoices. I spent most of the summer cutting open cardboard boxes with a Stanley knife. By the time October came around they were short-staffed on the shop floor. They put me out there. Once I figured out how to use the till I realised the job was a piece of piss. I wandered around in a nice warm shop surrounded by young women, put books on the shelves in alphabetical order, wore a shirt and trousers because I wanted to and it felt comfortable. But I soon realised that the people in the warehouse I'd worked in were brighter than those in both the shop and the university.

In the seminars hardly anyone who turned up had read the books. Those who did said the writers were boring. Afterwards they slagged off the lecturers. The big difference between the people in the warehouse and the people in the bookshop and the university was that in the warehouse they just said what they meant.

One morning I was arranging all the Kindles in a display on the front table near the entrance to the bookshop. Then I folded a dozen hooded tops with 'MMU' written on the front of them, putting them on the shelves where the German Literature section had once been. There was a display of science books in the front window, and a skeleton. A wino who looked like Dostoyevsky talked to the skeleton through the window.

A student came up to me. 'Hi,' he said, 'I'm looking for this book. I don't know the author's name or the title. But it's grey. It's a grey book. It's literally grey.' I asked him if he knew the ISBN number. He opened his mouth like a goldfish. I told him that without more information it would be hard for me to find the book on the computer. 'Oh my god,' he said, 'that's so rude,' before walking into Starbucks. Once a bloke came in and asked if we sold slippers. Someone else asked if they could leave their umbrella behind the till while they went into town.

I'd been brought up to say please and thank you. But after

a while I noticed that nobody ever said it back to me, either when I was working in the shop or standing at a bar. These fuckers thought I was being subservient when really it was just about manners. Twat after twat came in and dumped their book on the counter while talking away on their phones. I hated the way people acted on their phones, parading all their crap.

The bookshop was doing a roaring trade thanks to the Met discount card. It had been a genius idea and most of the senior staff got a year-end bonus. I didn't have a Met card. I wouldn't have thought to ask my parents to buy my course books. I got a staff discount and bought a number of books with that, then after a few months I just started nicking them.

The first time was on a Saturday. I wandered the shelves looking for books to take home. I put the books behind the counter and then left them on the desk there. And when nobody was around I put them in a carrier bag. At lunchtime, on my way home, I just picked up the bag and walked out of the door with it.

Back at the flat I opened a tin of all-day breakfast and put the contents in a pan on the hob, then filled a kettle and switched that on. Then I went into the living room and opened the bag of books. I loved the new-print smell of them, and the glossy covers, and I flicked through each of them in turn before piling them up on the coffee table. They had nobody on the door and never put tags in the books. There was nobody looking at CCTV cameras and they didn't record anything.

In the warehouse I stole a demolition hammer drill, just because I could. It took me years to sell the fucking thing. As a kid there used to be football stickers you could buy and then you stuck them in an album. There was a sweet shop called Dombovand's and I got caught stealing stickers from there. The old man just asked me to give them back and then when I did he clipped me across the back of the head and that was the end of that.

On Friday night we all went out to the Sandbar on Grosvenor Street. Twenty of us sat together along two long tables, all waffling away. I'm shy and I didn't like to go early. It was easier to stay until everyone else left, and in this way I drifted back into drinking.

Another night I saw a flyer on the table. I wandered over to The Salutation. People read their favourite poems by great writers, as well as their own, so it wasn't all shit. There was a man with a huge red beard, a middle-aged black fella, a couple of shy girls who were both trying to look like Audrey Hepburn, the fat MC called Fat MC who ran the night and read the best poems, a girl who read a poem about spunk in her hair, a bald man with part of his thumb missing who wrote in rhyme, a couple of bearded blokes in skinny jeans and suit jackets, and an assortment of golden drifters.

The Salutation went quiet as earnest young poets read out the magical words of Rimbaud, Verlaine, Bukowski, Bishop, Plath. I had by this time started to write little poems of my own. What appealed to me about writing was that you could work alone in a silent room. You had peace and quiet and nobody told you what to do. But this lot just wrote for applause.

One of the local drinkers from Hulme drifted in. Unlit roll-up tucked in the corner of his mouth, he stood there, frowning and swaying, before shouting, 'I saw the best minds of my generation, starving, hysterical, bollock naked, swinging

64

their cocks!' before walking through to the smoking area outside, a half-arsed affair of wicker and bonsai.

I was offered a full-time job in the bookshop and took it. At first I thought this would help with the tuition fees. And then I thought about all the loans I'd have to take out if I wanted to carry on. In the end I decided to fuck it off. I could just read the books at home. Those Tories were wankers for bringing tuition fees in.

On Saturday, when all the students had gone home and I floated around the bookshop pretending to tidy the shelves, I ended up chatting to John, a bald old guy who'd worked there for years on the top floor, selling all the boring books on business and marketing and computing.

'Dragging in here today,' I said.

'Don't wish your life away.'

'I'm not. I'm just saying it goes slow when the students aren't here.'

'You should be glad that life goes slow. Let me tell you.'

'Well, life doesn't go slow but working here does.'

'Your twenties will go quite quickly. Then your thirties will go even quicker. Forties in a flash. Fifties quicker than that. Before you know it you'll be my age.'

'Thanks for that.'

'No problem,' he said with a smile. Just then his wife came up the stairs. She was the assistant manager. John told me he had avoided any management responsibilities, even though they kept asking him.

'If you have nothing to do I can find you something,' she said.

'Excuse me?'

'I said I can find you something to do. And you, John.'

I wandered over to the shelves and started tidying the marketing books. There were thousands of marketing students at the university's business school, most of them from the Far East. One of the lecturers was a Korean woman with short black hair who came in the shop sometimes on her way to the car park. She had an American accent and said she liked my blue eyes.

I went down to the first floor. Wendy was in a room behind the till, sorting customer orders.

'Busy, Wendy?' I said.

'Busier than you.'

'Not difficult.'

'I know it isn't. What are you supposed to be doing?'

'Should be on my break.'

Wendy had paid off the mortgage on her house in East Levenshulme. I liked her. She took a train to Crosby on her days off and walked along the sands alone. She had long grey hair that she must have spent hours brushing. John said she'd had her heart broken by a Frenchman.

There was an author event. We'd ordered more copies of those books and I was in the staff room talking about the writers.

'I've read it. It was boring,' said John.

I'd read the book and wasn't bored. In fact, it was quite funny. This seemed unusual in literary fiction.

'You'll see what writers are like when he gets here. Up their own arse because they've had a book published.'

'I'm looking forward to it. I'm getting paid to listen to a reading. I've had worse jobs.'

'I've done a hundred and the novelty wears off, believe me. I mean, who gives a shit about what kind of chair a writer sits

66

in when they write? Or if they write with a pen or a pencil or on a laptop or a tablet or whatever. There's always someone asks that. I mean, who gives a shit? And people always ask, how much of you is in the character? How much of the story is real? Another daft question. It's fiction, you mugs. And we don't sell any more books than usual. These freeloaders come for the wine, flick through the books and fuck off. If they do buy them at all they get them cheaper off Amazon. I don't blame them either. You know, years ago I did this reading and it was the boxer Henry Cooper. And nobody else in the shop knew who he was. This was the guy who had knocked Muhammad Ali on his arse. 'Enry's 'Ammer, that's what they called his left hook. And I went into the staffroom before the reading and he was just sat there on his own. They'd left him on his own and he was flicking through a copy of the *Bookseller*. Now that is a boring magazine. But that was a good event, a proper event.'

The reading went well. Richard Ford was engaging, read beautifully despite the noise of the loudly humming fridge in Starbucks. We kept the door unlocked for latecomers, and a wino wandered in, stood there watching for a few minutes, then shook his head and walked back out again. Someone in the audience said, 'He's too late for the wine!' and everyone laughed. I felt like saying, 'Yes, you drank it all, you fat bastard.'

People milled around for what seemed like hours after the reading, drifting and talking bollocks. Even after I'd sold all we were going to sell and cleared the chairs away and taken the cash box back up to the safe upstairs you couldn't get them out. People will go to anything for free wine. They finally drifted off to the Deaf Institute for a drink but I was knackered and just went back to the flat.

After finishing my Saturday shift I walked home, cutting through the Science centre and halls of residence alongside it and skirting around the back of Odd Fellows Hall. There was a lull in the traffic on Upper Brook Street and on the Mancunian Way. I could hear crows calling from the tall trees around the flats. As I crossed at the traffic lights and made my way past the Manchester International College I noticed a wired-looking young man on the other side of the road near the Salvation Army. As I carried on walking I felt a hand grab my elbow. Then I saw the flash of a knife.

'Get over here,' he said, pushing me over to the grassy area at the back of the flats. Another lad turned up with a girl, and they stood next to us looking around. I could see they both had knives too. They were bread knives, about eight inches long and with serrated edges. 'How much money have you got,' said the first man with the knife. 'Give us your fucking money or I'll stab you.'

'I haven't got any money on me,' I said.

'Give us your fucking cash card then.'

I fished into my pocket and took out the card and when he asked me the pin number I made up a false one. He made me wait with the lad and the girl while he ran up to the Barclays cash point near the other end of Grosvenor Street. The lad pushed me down onto the grass and he and the girl stood over me. When the lad came back he looked crazy and said, 'Give me the fucking pin number now or I'll stick this fucking knife in your face.' I gave him the right number and I waited again with the lad and the girl. I looked up at the windows of the flats in which I lived. We were right outside. But why would you risk getting stabbed to help a stranger?

The following weekend in the shop I told my colleague

Tegan about it. She wasn't interested. It just made me look weak to her; I was the kind of man who could never make her feel safe. She had no compassion at all. I walked home that night with a knife in my own pocket, the same route as usual.

They took the maximum amount of cash out that day and I got it back from the bank. I also reported it to Longsight police who told me there had been a spate of such attacks on young men in the area. A few months later I was invited to look at an ID parade at Longsight station. A van came to the flats and picked me up, and there were half a dozen other lads in there. When it was my turn I picked out the two lads and the girl right away. The copper came up to me after and said I was the dog's bollocks for picking them out so quickly.

Not long after that there was a temporary girl who started working at the bookshop. She was more sympathetic when I told her about the mugging. She was from Leeds and had a broad Yorkshire accent. She also had large breasts. I was talking to her one time in the staff room and she went to the toilet. When she came back her nipples were bursting through the fabric of her blouse. She saw me looking at them and smiled. I asked her out and we had a drink in the Deaf Institute. When she got up to go to the toilet I gazed longingly at the weight of her breasts, and she came back to Lamport Court for the night. I never called her after that and she seemed fine about it. There was another girl around that time. I don't remember her name. It was in a bar called Joshua Brooks. All the women wore bright red lipstick and daft dresses. She took her bra off within minutes of us getting home. Her nipples were pierced and she had a tattoo of an eagle on the small of her back. When she'd got what she wanted she dressed and left. I didn't get laid that often and these things were minor triumphs for me.

My mate Jammo had always been a ladies' man. I'd played in the City youth team with him. He'd been a promising left winger but City let him go, and after spells at Bolton and Doncaster he jacked it in and began riding speedway bikes. After he'd ridden in a meeting at Belle Vue I met up with him in the Lass o'Gowrie.

It was a stop-start conversation, interrupted by Jammo going outside to smoke.

'How was it with the Aces then?' I asked him.

'Needs some investment that place. My old fella used to go there years ago. They used to get forty thousand watching the speedway and now there's one man and his dog. You know Paul Scholes goes there with his lad.'

'Red scum.'

'I know but you can't argue what a player he was.'

'Old news. All City now.'

'I know, mate. Great, isn't it? Pity we aren't a part of it. Anyway I prefer the speedway,' he said, a rueful smile on his face. He'd grown a beard and there was a grey patch on his chin.

'Where were you when that Agüero goal went in?'

'I was working overtime in a warehouse.'

'On your own?'

'More or less.'

'I was in this boozer in Flowery Field with my old fella. When the goal went in I've never seen anything like it. My old fella was on his knees in the middle of the pub, crying his eyes out. And he wasn't the only one. There were grown men all over the pub fucking balling. I was just laughing my bollocks off to be honest. It was weird though. When you saw those old blokes again, and when I saw my old fella again, they looked a bit sheepish. They were embarrassed about it. All those men fucking crying.'

'They had been waiting longer than us.'

'Yeah, I know what you mean. Imagine, though, if we'd have played against QPR.'

'Best not to think about it.'

'I know.'

'I always felt bad for you, mate, when they let you go.'

'Never had enough pace, did I?'

'You were a tricky little fucker though.'

'Too true. I nutmegged you in training enough times,' he said with a smile. 'Must have been harder for you though.'

'Don't know how I got through it.'

'Plaiting fog, mate, that's how we get through it. Plaiting fog. Sculpting haze and plaiting clouds and folding up the fucking mist. Scotch fucking mist. Anyway I'm going out for a smoke. You coming out?'

'No I'll stay here, mate.'

Dad took me to Maine Road. We parked right outside the Main Stand and just looked up at the height of it. The groundsman Stan Gibson walked in through an open gate but we didn't dare to follow. We walked all the way around the ground, past the North Stand, the brick walls and the blue turnstiles on the Kippax side, and then round to Platt Lane and back to the car. The ground was squeezed in between all these Coronation Street-style terraced houses. We got back in the car and as we drove away I looked back down the streets to see the curving roof of the Main Stand. I could see it at the end of each avenue. It was still there, street after street after street.

Ten years later I was still at home. In those days I took out on my mum what I couldn't so easily give back to my dad. And when I'd upset her, I'd go up to my room and listen to the Springsteen album, *Nebraska*.

On a Saturday night my dad used to sit on the couch in front of the TV, drinking cans of beer and reading the *Manchester Evening News Pink Final*. When we were kids he used to make this thing he called Rococo. He brought it in on a tray, and it consisted of peanuts, salted peanuts, and crisps – sometimes Monster Munch, sometimes Wotsits, sometimes Quavers, sometimes chip sticks – and we'd sit there watching telly, eating the Rococo before *Casualty* came on.

Lying on my bed I picked up the remote control for the stereo and played *Nebraska*. I looked at where the cat had sprayed one of the speakers, and also out of the window at the slate roof and chimney pot of the house opposite, and the telegraph pole with wires leading away from it. The song I loved most was called 'Used Cars'.

The Fiesta was my first car, and I got it from a showroom in Denton. Dad came with me and said it looked okay so I paid cash. A couple of days later it broke down because it needed a new alternator, but the bloke at the garage put a new one in without charging me.

I never washed it. Once I had an air freshener in the shape of a fir tree that hung from the rear-view mirror and smelled of coconut. The Fiesta broke down once when it overheated, and when I lifted the throbbing bonnet I realised that sometimes you had to put water in the engine.

Dad would drive us to Torquay for our holidays, the diesel Sierra noisily reliable for a round trip that must have been about eight hundred miles. Me and my brother would sit in the back and listen to our parents arguing about directions. Both my parents were smokers, and every now and then they'd light up and open their windows and the smoke would blow straight across us on the back seat. I liked the smell of my dad's Silk Cut more than my mum's Benson and Hedges, but I don't think my brother liked the smell of either. He'd never get car sick like I did. Every time we went to Torquay I vomited into a carrier bag and Mum binned it at the services.

Torquay was hot and full of palm trees and there was a big white footbridge that led across the road to the beach. We always went to a hotel with a swimming pool. I only learned to swim when I was eleven. I'd get sunburned playing football by the pool, and my hair went really blonde. To ease the pain of the sunburn in the evenings I'd roll a can of Coke across my arms and legs.

I met a Scottish kid called Alistair and kept having to ask him to repeat himself. He called me a 'Sassenach'. We went round the back of the hotel and into a garage and stole two bottles of Budweiser that we couldn't get the tops off. We had to smash them and drink carefully from the jagged necks. Then we threw the bottles over some tall trees and listened as they smashed onto the patio of the hotel next door.

That was the same holiday that I had my first kiss. There was a disco in the hotel and the girl smiled at me. Later on we watched *The X Factor* in the TV lounge. After that we went into the garden and sat with our feet in the pool. When her dad shouted her name she picked up her shoes then kissed me and ran off. I never saw her again because they left the next morning. I can't remember her name but her lips tasted of Opal Fruits. I think she was Alistair's sister.

The first car my dad ever had was a Ford Capri. It was red and he used to wash it every weekend. Then someone ploughed into it at a junction near Droylsden and it was a write-off. By the time he began taking me to the football he was driving the old blue Sierra. We'd park in one of the side streets off Platt Lane, and a local kid would ask if they could mind it. Dad always paid one of them but they were never there when we ran back to the car five minutes before the end of the match to avoid the traffic.

My Fiesta was red, but I wasn't bothered. It hid the rust better. One night it broke down on Ashton Old Road. It was rush hour and I stalled it in crawling traffic, and it wouldn't start again, and when I got out the cars behind me all began blowing their horns. I managed to push the car off the road by myself, and left it on the pavement with its hazard lights flashing near a bus stop where a bloke in a Belle Vue Aces jacket stood waiting.

I went into the Queen Anne and phoned my dad who came in the Sierra with a pair of jump leads, and we got the Fiesta going and I followed him home. The battery was flat and I'd flooded the engine by trying to start it over and over with the choke out.

Every night after work I parked next to Dad's Sierra at the front of the house. When Mum passed her test she bought herself a Mini and I had to park on the avenue around the corner. The small steering wheel of the Mini was like one on a Grand Prix game in an amusement arcade. The Mini got nicked from outside the house by a lad called Houghy I'd gone to school with. I began parking the Fiesta at the front again, and when Mum got the insurance she bought a silver Renault. One morning the next-door neighbour's daughter, who I could often hear through my bedroom wall having sex with the boyfriend she ended up marrying, drove her Volkswagen Golf straight into the back of Mum's Renault, while my Fiesta remained untouched around the corner.

Before I concentrated on football I'd been a good runner. There was the Mini Marathon at school. Our form set off running first, followed by the other five forms, then the second years, third years, fourth years and fifth years. A few days before, I'd cycled what I thought was the route with my dad, him on his racer and me on my red BMX from Asda.

After we'd all changed we walked out of school and down the road to the canal, then all had a number pinned to our red and white running vests. We stood around shivering and messing about until Mr Holt fired a starting gun. Within a few yards I turned around to see that some of my form had already been reduced to a walk – among them Monksy, who went on to be an insurance agent, Brownie, who managed an Asda, and Houghy, who nicked my mum's Mini.

I carried on running, my reflection keeping pace in the water. Soon enough all the runners had begun to spread apart and I was in the lead. I felt a little tightness in my chest and stopped spitting. A second wind came. I didn't look back until I knew nobody was there and then I turned to see the path and the green of the surrounding grass, curving away beside the flat water that darkened in the shade of a brick bridge. I passed a long stretch of muddy field where horses stood motionless. By Portland Basin I ran across the cobbles by a sad-looking man walking his dog, and a group of barges nestled by the towpath, and turned left to run towards Audenshaw, way above the Tame flowing in the valley below. The chill of the frost gave way to a lukewarm sun that spread through the sky. Water trickled down from the lock as I ran up and over a bridge on the bank. Swans stretched out their necks and hissed, while ducks jumped back into the water and glided slowly to the other side or curled up so their heads disappeared. Coming off the canal I looked at the bare trees. I went the wrong way and ran through terraced streets in Abbey Hey, past a chippy not yet open and a corner shop that looked more like a house. I disturbed a dozing tabby and he jumped off a garden wall. Turning around and going back past the corner shop I noticed one of the marshals of the race, Slogger Delaney, sat on a chair on the other side of the road, smoking a cigarette, yellow flag resting across his lap.

Soon I began the homeward stretch, back through Audenshaw and the streets I grew up on. I ran past the sloping banks of the reservoirs and along Stamford Road and cut through a stretch of wasteland past an overhanging tree with a rope swing. I carried on past the shop, where a lad stood leaning near the window smoking, one leg tucked up behind him against the wall.

I ran in through the school gates and was about to begin the last bit of the race, a lap of the school field, when I heard voices getting louder from behind. Running four abreast, lads from the fifth year came fast approaching, seemingly without effort at a time when I was beginning to flag. I looked ahead at the red cones that marked the remainder of the route across the field and, passing the basketball courts and behind the first set of rugby posts, the voices behind me got louder and louder until the group of four finally passed.

None of them even seemed to be breathing heavily. They all

ran for East Cheshire Harriers. I looked around and nobody else was coming. The four ahead of me stretched away and I saw as they all crossed the line together. As I passed behind the last of the rugby posts and began my own final stretch, I saw my dad sitting on his bike, on the other side of the school railings. I sprinted the last bit and ran over the finishing line before doubling back to show my number to Paul Dalton, who sat with a pen and paper behind a desk moved out onto the grass, his broken leg propped up in the mud.

Tegan from the bookshop organised a party for her birthday on a Saturday night. After work me and John got on the 43 and headed down Wilmslow Road to the leafy suburbs of Didsbury. We looked from the windows as the bus passed along the Curry Mile in Rusholme, then the old Fallowfield train station next to Sainsbury's, and on through Withington and past the hospital until we got off near Lapwing Lane. We had a pint in the Metropolitan and then another in the Railway, before wandering the short distance to the flat on Old Lansdowne Road. It was a beautiful old Victorian house and we trailed up two flights of stairs to the flat. When Tegan welcomed us inside we were met by the sound of Cuban music. It was a cocktails-themed party and I tried a White Russian.

Between drinks I looked around at the room. People stood around talking politely to each other and sipping their drinks. There were loads of different people there, and only a handful from the bookshop.

A woman with big black-rimmed glasses, bright-red lipstick and a long floral dress was introduced to me by John.

'What do you do?' she said.

'I just work in the bookshop.'

'Of course, I know that. Tegan works in the bookshop but she's an art historian.'

'I just work in the bookshop. I'm going for a beer. Do you want one?' I asked, brushing past her.

'Don't touch me,' she said.

I stood in the kitchen for a while trying to keep pace with the drinking of a couple of fat blokes, and then got myself another can of lager from the fridge. I spoke to someone in the doorway but she just walked off and so I wandered my way down the stairs and out into the back garden. It was a beautiful night, just the faint sounds of the Cuban music drifting down to the moonlit garden. A fox trotted across the grass and a burglar light came on. The fox turned and looked right at me. I lay on the grass and held the beer can to my chest while looking up at the moon. I thought Tegan might come down but she didn't. Later I heard people leaving. I got up off the grass, taking my empty can and putting it in a wheelie bin before making my way back upstairs to the flat. The music had stopped playing and Tegan and her bearded boyfriend were tidying up. I walked past them to the kitchen and fished in the fridge for another beer. There were plenty of cans left and I figured the party wasn't over until all the beer had gone. I walked back into the living room and slumped on the couch as Tegan and her boyfriend continued to tidy.

'Just leave it until the morning,' I said.

'We'll do it now, thanks,' said Tegan.

'You don't mind me having another beer?'

'You have all the beer you want, man,' said the boyfriend.

'Cheers. What's your name anyway, chief?'

'Ludo.'

'Okay, chief.'

'Tegan introduced us before.'

'Hey, no problem, chief.' I could see he hated being called chief. I gulped down my beer and went back into the kitchen for another. I heard them talking in the living room.

'Listen, man, why don't you take that one with you?'

'Yeah, no problem, chief.' I got up and was going to shake his hand but he carried on tidying. Neither of them said anything as I walked out of the door.

I went back into the garden. The early morning sun shone through the branches of tall trees. I looked around for the fox then walked home down Wilmslow Road.

The following week I was sitting in the precinct centre having my lunch when a wino walked up to me. It was the guy I'd seen talking to the skeleton who looked like Dostoyevsky, with a bald head and a snub nose and a long wispy beard. I'd read *Crime and Punishment*. In *Crime and Punishment* the central character Raskolnikov kills someone at the start and then bangs on about it for five hundred pages. I'd nicked it from the shop. John said the wino had been a professor at the university.

'You having a good day?' he said to me.

'Not especially.'

'Come on. You're having a good day. Good for you, lad.'

'Are you a professor then?'

His blue eyes glistened. 'Used to be.'

'What subject?'

'Romantic literature. Oh yes. Where is he, the champion and the child of all that's great or little, wise or wild? Whose game was empires, and whose stakes were thrones. Whose table earth – whose dice were human bones?'

'What's that from?'

'What's that from? Ha ha ha ha ha, you stupid bastard!'

79

'Bit harsh.'

'Byron.'

'Right. I'll have to look it up.'

'Romance is dead. Get back on your phone. I was married once, you know. Are you married? I was married. But she didn't like me drinking. I said I can't be tamed. And I like women as well, you see. One woman is not enough for a man like me.'

'You got any kids?'

'Two lads. Little bastards they are. Hate me. It was my birthday last week and nothing from them. Manchester University. Nothing from them either.'

'Why aren't you at the university any more?'

'I told you I liked the ladies, didn't I? Still do. Had a second year. Here darling,' he said, grabbing the jacket of a young woman as she walked by.

'You can't do that, mate,' I said.

'Relax, will you. Eat, drink and love. The rest isn't worth a fuck. Everyone is so uptight these days. I was married, you know. But she didn't like me drinking. I can't be tamed. I can't be tamed me,' he said, drinking from his bottle of cheap cider. 'Look, I don't like to ask and I know you're having your lunch but can you spare us a little bit of change, lad, just for a cup of tea?'

I gave him all the change I had. I don't know why. I was such a mug sometimes. He turned up in the precinct centre again, not long after that. He clearly had no memory of speaking to me before. I didn't ask him if he'd been a professor, but he said, 'Where is he, the champion and the child of all that's great or little, wise or wild. Whose game was empires, and whose stakes were thrones. Whose table earth – whose dice were human bones?' Then he said, 'I was married. But she didn't like me drinking. I can't be tamed. I love women.' As I finished my sandwich he said, 'Look, I know you're having your lunch, lad, but can you spare us a bit of change for a cup of tea?' Again I gave him what change I had and he said, 'Eat, drink and love. The rest isn't worth a fuck.'

In the afternoon a student with one side of his head shaved broke away from a mobile phone conversation and said, 'Hi there, fella, I'm after this book, it's called 1984, but I don't know who it's by.'

'You don't . . . err . . . yeah . . . I think we've got a copy in. I'll just look.' Expecting the customer to follow I turned around to see that he was leaning on the counter and had resumed his conversation on the phone.

'Is that the one?' I asked, putting the book down on the counter.

'Hang on, fella . . . err, yeah that must be it. There aren't any with the same title are there?'

'No, chief. This is the one you want.'

When John came down to check how I was doing I told him about the student and 1984.

'You get that all the time.'

After that there were no customers for a while. I sat behind the till, reading the Ricky Hatton autobiography I'd picked up from the music section. Getting beat fucked him up and then he'd fallen out with his family. It was a sad story.

Later that summer the big knobs at the bookshop put us on a course called 'Investors in Performance'. It was something they came up with in the wake of the rise of internet shopping, and the premise was that shops had the potential advantage in terms of customer service.

At a big old house in Rusholme we all trailed to our tables. Everyone was given a big bottle of water to help with hydration, and every five minutes someone went for a slash. The morning was spent going through the health and safety regulations of the house that we'd be spending a total of five hours in. Then there were all the introductions, where everyone present was made to feel valued and at ease.

After a lunch of stuffed peppers each table had to think of a good example of customer service, and after that the presenters came up with an exercise to highlight the value of positive thinking. A volunteer was found from the audience of booksellers and each table was asked to try and lift him out of his chair using only their thumbs. Nobody could do it because, like the presenter said, they didn't expect to be able to. But when the presenters tried, using both their thumbs and shoulders, they succeeded. People gasped, and then applauded.

Before the applause died down John got up and walked out, muttering 'Bollocks'. Everyone watched him standing on the patio. Some people even booed him as he shook his head and lit a fag. Because of the direction of the breeze, some of the smoke blew into the room. A couple of the booksellers covered their mouths with their hands and one said that she was going to faint unless the door was closed.

I watched as the presenters looked momentarily shattered. After a brief conference, one of them announced that it was exactly John's kind of attitude that this seminar was hoping to eradicate. People clapped at this.

At the end of the seminar, after everyone had hugged each other, I walked outside and went to the Ford Madox Brown with John.

'That was funny,' I said.

'Give me strength. The world is fucking mad. These people don't know anything. When someone goes into a bookshop they don't want to be met by some grinning idiot with a laminated sign swinging from their neck saying "Happy to Help". You go into a bookshop for a bit of peace and quiet. These conceited graduates who can't get a job anywhere else, fuck me. They have to try and make the job seem more important than it is. A bookshop is a bookshop is a bookshop, no matter how much you make of it. "Booksellers", we're all "booksellers", they say. They aren't, they're till jockeys, no more, no less. People like me, who've actually been working in the bookshop for a few years and know virtually every book we have in the shop – that's not good enough because I don't smile back at some twat on a mobile phone pointing at a book he wants me to get for him off the shelf. They want a rapid turnover of vapid cretins. They don't value wisdom, experience, someone who's read hundreds of novels. They want someone who can display the autobiography of a footballer or a bird with fake tits in a swirling fan across a front table that a publisher has paid to have it on. It's horseshit. All I do these days is fold fucking sweaters.'

'It was great when you went outside. You should have said something though. It would have been funny.'

'Do you realise how many of these things I've been on over the years? They don't even listen to me any more. They just smile at me because they've been told what to expect. They think "Oh, it's just John".' Why do you think I'm only the floor manager? I could run our shop in my sleep, better than that fuckwit who's in charge at the moment. Do you know what she reads? Fucking Harry Potter and Lord of the Rings. I read Lord of the Rings when I was about twelve. She's never read

Hamsun or Huysmans or Houellebecq and she's in charge of the shop. She's a brown-tonguing bastard as brainwashed as all the rest. She doesn't care what people are reading. She's all about sales figures and her own promotion to one of the big branches in Oxford.'

'Pint?'

'Too *fucking* right.'

I came back with the pints. Then he started banging on about the bedroom tax the Tories had brought in.

'My mate has cerebral palsy and his wife and kids left him so he's got two spare bedrooms. But he spent twenty years adapting the house and it has ramps for his wheelchair, and there's a stairlift and a disabled shower.'

'Well, wherever they move him they'll have to fit those things in, won't they?'

'That's the joke. They won't save any money because they'll have to adapt wherever he moves to. And there aren't hardly any one-bedroom places around there.'

'There must be better ways of saving money than taking it off the disabled.'

'He went sixty quid behind on the rent and the twats at the council sent him a threatening letter about taking him to court. There's a neighbour on our street, Jenny, and I went to school with her. She's lived in that same house all her life, she stayed there when her parents died. She's never lived anywhere else and now she's having to move out as well because they've cut her benefits right down and she can't afford to stay there any more.'

'Cunts.'

'It is totally unfair. There are thousands of people who really need these benefits. What would you rather have, a system that

84

provides for those that need it, or a system that makes sure nobody is taking the piss? I'd rather make sure the poor and disabled get looked after, rather than penalising them because of benefit cheats. Get some money off the fucking bankers, tax the rich twats. If you're rich then you can spare it. Take ten per cent off their fucking weekly wage. What's a hundred quid a week when you're getting a thousand? Not the same as ten quid a week when you're getting a hundred, is it? And they slag them off for smoking and drinking. These rich fuckers aren't in the real world. When you don't have anything in your life then smoking and drinking is the only pleasure you have. Anyway I'm going out for a smoke,' he said, zipping up his coat and walking out through the fire exit. I looked at him through the glass. He stood there chatting to other smokers as the wind whipped at their jackets and the smoke swirled away into the night.

The next day, after selling a copy of a ghost-written celebrity autobiography and a yellow, fish-shaped radio to a man wearing a T-shirt with a logo on it that read 'I'M WORTH IT', I looked outside the window and saw Dostoyevsky pushing a shopping trolley. He wore a beige suit and had a can of lager in his hand. A few minutes later he wheeled the trolley into the shop. It was full of dirty dolls and figurines, and surrounding them were 'No Smoking' signs of all different shapes and sizes.

'What's with the dolls?' I asked.

'You wouldn't understand, lad.'

'I might do.'

'You wouldn't.'

'Try me. I'm interested.'

'Oh fuck off,' he said, wheeling his trolley out of the shop.

I went back to the till. Tegan told me that she and Ludo

had been going down to Barton Moss in Salford every day to protest about fracking.

'I was there yesterday and they beat the shit out of this guy,' she said.

'Really?'

'Yeah, beat the shit out of him. Those pigs.'

'He must have been doing something to wind them up.'

'Wake up, will you? You don't know what these pigs are like.'

'I've had mixed experiences, I have to say.'

'But you've never protested against anything, have you? Where's your backbone?'

'Look, you've got the moral high ground. And you are welcome to it, okay? I don't give a fuck. I don't know enough about it. It's like when they all come down Oxford Road banging on about Palestine. What the fuck is that to do with us?'

There was a customer waiting. I looked at Tegan but she just carried on talking. 'How would you feel if another country took your land away and persecuted your people?'

'My ancestors are Scottish.'

'Oh be serious.'

'I am being serious.'

'Freedom for Palestine is crucial.'

'Nothing to do with me.'

'That's naive.'

'Look, you protest for these things because it makes you feel better about yourself.'

'What?' she said, her face reddening.

'You've got a double-barrelled surname. Since when have you had to struggle for anything?'

'You've got no idea, have you?'

'Obviously touched a nerve.'

'Just because I've got a double-barrelled surname doesn't mean I've got money. My father was out of work on and off most of the time when I was growing up and we had to live on my mother's wages. That's just inverted snobbery.'

'Bet you had to sell some fucking chandeliers, did you? Or let one of the maids go? Sack the butler?'

'That's not even funny. You are horrible.'

I served the customer and then went on my break. I'd had enough.

I was watching the telly that night and this psychic called Derek Acorah came on. Two ladies in the audience looked on in awe as Acorah told them about their deceased. He said, 'I'm hearing Bill, Billy?' and the ladies nodded. 'Always had a bad back, is that right? He wants you to know that he is watching over you.' The ladies smiled and looked at each other, and there were gentle murmurs of appreciation from the audience. There was subtle, dreamy music on in the background.

I went on to YouTube and found some clips of past-life regressions, done by a gorgeous blonde woman called Andrea Foulkes. When she induced people into a hypnotic state I found her voice really calming. And of course her tits were huge. I watched one clip after another until I felt completely serene. I saved all of these clips on my phone, and at the times when I felt like getting pissed I watched them instead. For a while it worked. Then I just went to the pub again.

I had always had a thing about barmaids. It's not hard to work out why. There was something about the way they pulled back the pump to fill the pints and the fact that you were always drunk when you saw them. When everyone from the bookshop had gone back home to Didsbury and Chorlton I sat at the bar, drinking on my own. Eventually I told the barmaid I'd played for City and she laughed like she'd heard it all before.

It made me laugh when I went out in places like West Didsbury and Chorlton. The men had moisturised beards and spotless retro trainers and skinny jeans. And they rode around on expensive bicycles made by Dawes, and wore horn-rimmed specs they didn't need for seeing, and they never got drunk. When you tried talking to them they sat there silently. I didn't know how to talk to men like that. Men who'd burst into tears after five minutes of manual labour. They sat outside bars called Folk and the Art of Tea, smoking roll-ups and sipping Belgian beer as the buses and taxis thundered past along the busy main road. Burton Road in West Didsbury was lined with restaurants and boutiques, and you'd see people who'd been famous in the 90s, grown older and pushing prams, and dropping their kids off at Cavendish Road.

People who had moved to Chorlton called themselves 'Chorltonistas' and referred to Chorlton as 'Chorltonia'. Nobody else gave a fuck. They had a vegetarian supermarket there called The Unicorn which just about sums the place up.

I had a drink one night after work with Tegan, John and Rhiannon. Rhiannon lived near Burton Road so we got in a taxi on Oxford Road and headed there. Long after they'd gone home I was drinking on my own in a bar called Mary and Archie. I got talking to this bloke and his mate. The bar staff seemed more relaxed than they'd been when I was sitting on my own. One of these blokes said he was the writer J.H. Bounds, as though I should have heard of him. We were all drinking expensive German beer. Vomiting juice.

I'd read Nabokov and we started talking about *Pnin*. And

this J.H. Bounds had obviously never read it because when I asked him about the novel he just covered his arse by talking in general terms. The most important thing for him was how you said 'Pnin'. He corrected me but I kept saying it the same. We both said 'p' the same way but I said 'nin' as in 'bin' and he said 'neen' as in 'been'. J.H. got more and more exasperated and eventually started to ignore me. There were three of us sat at the table but he just talked to his mate. I necked my beer and got up to leave, but before I did I looked at J.H. Bounds and his ridiculous handlebar moustache. I reached over to twist either end of it but he pushed me away and then the bar staff asked me to leave.

I walked the long way home, wandering down Fog Lane and through Burnage. I saw the Sifters record shop where Noel Gallagher used to go. Hard to believe two brothers from Burnage went on to be in the biggest band in the world. They were City fans too. I took a left onto Kingsway and kept walking, past the B&Q and on towards home.

We were all going to the park. I walked through the long grass beside the back path that paralleled the train line and led to Guide Bridge station. I ducked down and hid from my brother. I crawled on my hands and knees through the tall grass and sneaked up on him, and when he ran away laughing I lay back briefly and squinted at the sun.

The train took us over the Dinting viaduct and I looked down at a tiny football pitch and when we got off at Glossop we made the short walk to Manor Park. Dad took the football out of the carrier bag and we ran on to the grass to play. We used two saplings as our goal posts and Dad crossed the ball over time and again for me and my brother to head or volley it between the budding trees. We got chips from the chippy and ice creams from the van, and paddled in the freezing stream and trundled around on the miniature railway or just sat on benches in the sun.

On the way home, the early evening sunlight spread across fields that had once been landfill. Tall grass surrounded a pond where frogspawn dazzled. The grass was a deep green and the crows flying above it a glossy black. I crawled through the tall grass and lay back looking up at the blue sky until my dad shouted me and I got up and ran past the red bricks of the railway bridge.

The day after, I scratched at the ant bites on my arms and legs and felt my face still glowing from the sun. I took the football out onto the fields where they'd cut the grass. My brother didn't want to play and stayed inside drawing pictures. I made goals from piles of cuttings, and dribbled between saplings, and covered miles of ground running across the fields with my football. I played keepy-uppy until the strength was gone from my legs and I made my way back home across the railway bridge and down the path and in through the back gate. The cats were blinking and lounging on the lawn. The patio door was open and knives, forks and spoons were shining on the table.

A dream that had appeared to be coming true had been taken away by a bad landing after a tackle, a twist of my cruciate ligaments that changed my future, took away my speed and specialness. The masses should have been watching me with my two good feet and my finishing instincts and my wide range of passing. Now I was among them watching others. How easy it would have been, after all those hours playing on top of landfill, to grace the spotless pitches of the Premier

League. I'd interchange passes with Agüero, run into the box and meet his return pass, hear that split-second sound of the ball hitting the net before the rise of the Etihad roar.

Sitting in Albert Square one spring evening, pleasantly sloshed, I looked up at the clock tower of the Town Hall. It was a building I'd always loved to look at, except at Christmas when they put a daft inflatable Santa on the front of it and wasted thousands on fireworks. I had been drinking in a bar called Cellar Vie with Scoie because they had lager on at two quid a pint, and when he went wandering back up to Piccadilly to get on the tram back to Droylsden I sat on a bench in Albert Square, the last of the sun shining on the Town Hall clock tower. There were hardly any people around and the traffic noise was minimal. I leaned my head back to look up at the sky and I saw what looked like a white bird with bits of grey on it. When it flew at a certain angle the last of the evening sun shone on its yellow talons. It sat on a little wall above the clock face, its head nervously looking around. I hoped it would lift off again to fly, but it just sat there until dark. I wandered off in the direction of Princess Street.

The following morning I looked on Google at various pictures of birds of prey and judging by the colour of its feathers I reckoned I'd been watching a peregrine falcon. There were a few of them nesting in high buildings around Manchester, on top of the CIS building, the Arndale and the cathedral, and every time I was in town from then on I'd look up into the sky for them.

When I was a kid I had a mate called Keith. His parents had got divorced when his mum hooked up with this bloke who worked on oil rigs in the North Sea. His dad was so pissed off that he moved to the Isle of Arran. He lived in

Shiskine, and published a book every year that recorded all the bird sightings on the island. Every summer Keith used to go to Arran, and one year it was all set up that I was going to go with him. But for reasons I don't remember it never happened.

It was after having a pint with Scoie in the Wetherspoon's near St Peter's Square that I first thought of going camping on my own. Since he'd got married, Scoie had been all over Britain and Ireland with his Mrs, staying in a tent on camp sites. He kept putting the pictures on Facebook.

They didn't have any tents in the Cotswold camping shop on Oxford Road so I got on my bike and cycled to the Go Outdoors in Stockport. I picked up a two-man Coleman Cobra for sixty quid, and then the next day I booked some train tickets from Piccadilly to Ardrossan Harbour.

Getting off the train at Ardrossan I walked under a covered walkway to the ticket office. Climbing on the ferry I went and sat at what I thought was the front, realising after the ferry had turned around that I was at the back. In the cafe four members of staff stood waiting for the ferry passengers. Some passengers went to the cafe, others to the lounge at the front of the boat, others to sit in rows of chairs facing forwards. I went into the shop and bought myself the Ordnance Survey map for the island. After unfolding it and having a quick look I folded it back up and put it into the rucksack I'd left in a storage area near the boarding point.

On deck the wind off the water was strong and I adjusted my cap to make it tighter. I put my sunglasses on and stood at the front of the boat watching as the mountains of the island became bigger. Looking at them felt like being in a different world. Gulls flew above the boat, occasionally swooping down close to people eating snacks in the seating area at the back. There was the salt smell off the sea and the spray of water in the breeze.

As we approached Brodick harbour I went downstairs for my rucksack. A man opened the ferry doors and there was a scrum to get off. We all shuffled down a gangway that was split in half by a white barrier. One half of the gangway was wider than the other. I trundled down the wide side with my rucksack, the sleeping mat sticking out behind me. There was a long line of people waiting to board the ferry. People constantly pushed into my rucksack as though I couldn't feel it. Outside the ticket office in Brodick there was a little bus station and I was one of the first to get on the 323 to Lamlash. The bus was there for a good fifteen minutes and was jam packed by the time we started the steep ascent up the hill.

As the bus reached the crest of the hill a view opened up over Lamlash Bay, with Holy Isle right there in the middle of the water. The beauty of the scene was breathtaking. I looked around the bus and the eyes of other tourists were also glazed in wonder.

As the bus sped down the hill and turned right into Lamlash we were almost by the water's edge. There were numerous yachts and boats anchored in the sparkling bay. We passed a few pubs along the road and I got out opposite a place called The Ship House. On a bench overlooking the bay I took the map from my rucksack and traced the road with my finger towards the campsite at Cordon. The beauty of Holy Isle sitting in the bay was something else, its green bulk rising to a summit called Mullach Mor. There was a tiny lighthouse at the southern end of the island. I sat on that bench for a long time, wondering why people lived in cities.

Putting my rucksack back on I continued along the coastline, passing a playground and a tennis court, and a parking area where an old man and his wife sat in a caravan staring out at the view of Holy Isle. A man in a straw boater walked a sausage dog along the beach. There was a sign at the back of the tennis court for the campsite. The footpath crossed a wooden footbridge over a burn and then led to a road with a little terrace of houses. On the garage roof of the end terrace there was a heron looking out to where the burn entered the bay. It was a golden evening but I was knackered. At the campsite I put up my tent and had an early night.

The next morning I went to the Ship House. It was a gift shop just down from the Co-op and overlooking the bay in Lamlash. There were two sides to the shop. In one side where the little craggy-faced owner stood behind the counter it was like a paper shop, where they had *The Arran Banner* and other newspapers, and cigarettes. There were all other kinds of bric-a-brac that might be useful to campers and tourists like camping fuel for stoves, lighters, matches, inflatable mattresses, cans of beans, packets of biscuits, chocolate, crisps, sun hats, sun cream, midge repellent, pain killers, key rings, pens. There were racks of postcards in there too, with views of Brodick Bay, Brodick Castle, Holy Isle, the Sleeping Giant, Lochranza Castle, Ailsa Craig, Whiting Bay and Glenashdale Falls. I bought one with a picture of the mountain Cir Mhor. I also bought a canister of camping gas and a souvenir mug. When I paid for them the owner was radiant, smiling, welcoming, his craggy face beaming.

Strong sunlight kept the midges off as did the breeze that flooded through the campsite off the bay. Two young women turned up and parked their car right next to me. I watched as they huffed and sweated putting up their two-person tent. I offered to help but they said they were fine. When they eventually had the tent up they folded out two chairs and sat there smoking cigarettes and drinking cans of lager.

I went out for a walk in the afternoon, pausing where the burn entered the bay. Right by the waterline a tiny white bird with a black ring around its neck called loudly. Later on I followed the coast road past Margnaheglish. In the garden of a house called Seabank I saw a man playing acoustic guitar and lots of men and women sitting cross legged on the lawn, drinking beer and wine and writing in little coloured notebooks. The tide was in and the waters of the bay lapped against the shore to the accompaniment of Neil Young's 'Heart of Gold'. A bird sat at the shoreline, unfolding. I asked an old bloke passing along the road if he knew what it was and he told me it was a cormorant or a shag, he didn't know which. In the garden of the house two young men started throwing a Frisbee to each other, trying to catch it while still holding their cans of beer. I watched them a while and they kept catching the Frisbee, only slightly spilling beer until one of them chased the Frisbee head first into the privet hedge, throwing his beer can into the air and crashing to a sudden halt. The football sat ignored on the lawn.

In the sunlight shining across the bay a group of eight birds flew exuberantly over the water, the black and white of their feathers dazzling. I walked on a little sadly because I didn't know what they were. From the Clauchland Hills I took in the sunlit views of Holy Isle and followed the Brodick Road to drop back down into Lamlash. I popped into the Pierhead Tavern for a swift pint, sitting outside and watching the life of Lamlash before heading back to the campsite.

Many more tents had gone up during the day and I was glad of my quiet position at the far end of the campsite. The two women didn't seem to be in their tent and I dropped easily off to sleep only to be woken by them a couple of hours later. It sounded like they had two lads with them. It went briefly quiet and then the sounds of sex began. They must have been having sex right next to each other in the two-person tent and I lay there unable to escape the sounds. The lads made most of the noise and then left. After that the girls giggled to each other and talked for hours.

In the morning I went to the laundry room to wash my sweaty clothes. It was another hot day so I sat there in the shade, just wearing my shorts. A young girl came in to take washing out of one of the other machines and seemed painfully shy. Her mother came in and smiled warmly at me before helping her daughter with the clothes.

As I watched the red light click on to 'rinse', a big old man came in and started talking to me as he washed two white cups in the sink. He had massive shoulders and piles of white hair on his chest. Even his pot belly looked muscular.

'You know I used to be world champion?' he said, looking at me with bright, sky-blue eyes.

'Really?'

'Yep. Wrestling. Used to drive up and down the country. Once I drove from Glasgow to Inverness and back on the same day and then got up for work in the morning!'

'Wow. That's a long drive.'

'It was. Happy days though. Mick McManus, Big Daddy, Giant Haystacks, Kendo Nagasaki. I beat them all at one time or another.'

'It was big in those days, wasn't it?'

'Another time I drove down to Birmingham and back on the same day. Manchester, Liverpool, Hull. I used to drive everywhere.'

'I'm from Manchester.'

'Yep. World champion I was. Anyway, nice to meet you,' he said, and with that he left, carrying his two white cups.

More than once on the campsite I had old men come up to me and talk to me like that. And men of my own age too. They saw that I was camping on my own. I reminded the old men of when they were young and the young men of when they were free.

In the morning I left for Lochranza, the village at the north end of the island. After putting up my tent at the campsite there I walked along the coastal road heading for the Cock of Arran. I was getting better at reading the map. It was a still morning with haze above the waters of the Firth of Clyde and the Sound of Bute. I passed South Newton and reached Newton Point, the road becoming a cart track and then a footpath among a collection of coastal rocks. At Fairy Dell I sat on the shoreline and took off my boots to soothe my knee in the water. Three men in yellow kayaks passed in silence save for the gentle slapping of their paddles. A couple walked their dog down the footpath from the Knowe. I put my socks and boots back on and turned to see a pair of bright little birds in Fairy Dell, the tuft of red on their heads quite beautiful.

Continuing around the headland I reached the giant sandstone rock and looked out again at the calm waters of the Sound of Bute. On a rock sticking out of the water a seal basked in the morning sunlight. I took out my binoculars to look at it more closely and saw it yawning and blinking its eyes. It heard me as I walked along the rocks by the shoreline and kept turning its head to look around, but it couldn't be bothered to slide off the rock. I passed Ossian's Cave as I walked through woodland to finally reach the croft at Laggan marked on the map. The little white building staring out towards the haze covering the Firth of Clyde had shutters on its front windows. I sat on the step and leaned against the sky-blue door, caught in a mid-morning sun trap, only to be set upon by horse flies. I had sprayed all my exposed skin with midge spray and this seemed to keep the horse flies off, but instead they landed on my shoulders and bit through my T-shirt, sharp little bites that came a second or two after they'd landed. Just then the door of the cottage opened.

'Are you comfy on my doorstep?' said a little old lady with a shock of white hair. 'Come in so I can close the door and keep the flies out.'

I dragged my rucksack in through the door. There was one big room with an open fire at one end and a stove at the other. Light shone in through the windows at the back and two skylights in the ceiling. I saw through one of the windows that there was a garden at the back.

'You're the first one to sit on the doorstep for a long time,' she said, taking off her wire-rimmed glasses and rubbing her eyes. 'I hear people going past, but people don't stop here as much as they used to. I suppose you'll be taking the path at the back and going over to Chalmadale?'

'Yes, that will take me back to Lochranza, won't it?'

'It would do, yes, that's right. It would do.'

When the water boiled on the stove she poured it into two metal cups before passing one to me. There had been no option of milk or sugar. I looked at the end of the room where the kitchen was and couldn't see a fridge. There was a large candlestick on the dining table and a tiny transistor radio on the bookshelf. I stood up to take a look at the books and saw that the shelves were filled almost entirely by the work of a writer called Seton Gordon.

'You like this Seton Gordon then?'

'Who?'

'Seton Gordon.'

'All the books belong to Cameron.'

'Cameron?'

'My husband. He'll be on his way back for lunch soon. He's away at the sheep pens.'

'Oh right.'

'Seton Gordon. Yes, I did read some of them books years ago. He didn't write much about Arran. It was mainly the Cairngorms and Skye. And golden eagles. He liked golden eagles.'

'Well, thank you for the tea,' I said, hesitating at the thought of the horse flies.

'Stay for another cup,' she said, 'Cameron will be back soon.'

When Cameron arrived he looked pleasantly surprised. A tiny little man with a bald head and round glasses just like those of his wife, he wore a tweed jacket and long waterproof trousers. He must have been hot. He passed me another mug of black tea, sipped from his own and started talking.

'We used to own the newsagents in Whiting Bay, didn't we, Annie? One night we got robbed. The alarms were going and I went out across the road and there were three men in a boat rowing away. They came from Saltcoats. They'd rowed all the way over to rob our shop. After that we sold up and decided to come up here. This croft was going for a song. Lochranza is like a different country compared to Whiting Bay. We're never going down south again, are we, love?'

'Not while I'm still living.'

'Lochranza probably gets more rain but we've got all the deer here and that view out the front there. There's nobody going to be robbing us in a fishing boat coming that way. Not even from Millport. Have you seen the deer?'

'I think there was one on the golf course next to the campsite.'

'Aye, you get them there. But when you walk up to the top of the hill up here you should see them. There's plenty, and don't be scared of them, they won't do you any harm. But watch out for those horse flies. I know it's hot but put your jacket on over your T-shirt there. That should keep them off.'

He gulped his tea down and said, 'Do you know that Annie has got an MBE for her services to Scottish country dancing?'

'Really?'

'Oh, aye. Look,' he said, pointing to the MBE standing proudly on the fireplace.

'Do you not feel a bit lonely here?'

'Not at all. We've got our little boat, and we can walk along the coastal path to Lochranza or take the path over the hill. And you'll have been past Fairy Dell. There's another path there.'

'Should we tell him about Fairy Dell?' said Annie.

'Tell him what? The best thing is to show people, not tell them. We could walk out there tonight and then you can come back here and stay until the morning.'

'Err . . .'

'It would be a treat for us,' she said. 'We don't get much by way of company any more.'

'Annie, let's go to Fairy Dell. You can leave your rucksack here,' he said, looking at me with a smile.

By now it was mid-afternoon. We followed the path back past Ossian's Cave and the giant sandstone rock that Cameron said was the Cock of Arran. By now the path was right by the water's edge and the seal's rock was submerged.

At Fairy Dell water fell down the hillside and trickled over pebbles to the shore. The air was filled with the reddish birds I'd seen before. Annie told me they were lesser redpolls, dozens of them, swirling and circling. I looked at Annie and she was beaming, and Cameron smiled and held her hand as we all watched the spectacle of the redpolls. Annie's eyes were glowing, just like mine. Cameron's were the same too. The redpolls contrasted with a flash of yellow, a yellowhammer singing and flying, and we sat down on shoreline rocks just listening and watching as the songs of the birds mixed with the sounds of the water.

'And you know there is also something special around this corner too,' said Cameron, his glasses sparkling as he walked on.

Further around the shoreline Cameron pointed to the rocks there. 'This is where Hutton came up with his theory of the earth. You see those rocks there? You see how these ones at the front point one way, and the ones behind it point the other way? That's "Hutton's Unconformity".' These rocks at the front are five hundred million years old, and the ones behind it, the sandstone, they are three hundred million years old. You can go your own way. You don't have to be like everyone else. Millions of years between them. Birds, unconformity, nature, I mean, look at this place! And you haven't seen the deer yet.'

He kissed Annie again and I followed them back to their isolated cottage. I thought of telling them that I'd played for City but it seemed like an irrelevance. Darkness was falling and I knew there wouldn't be a great deal of privacy that night. But the warmth of this couple relaxed me, as did the sound of the Firth lapping gently at the shore and the coastal birds calling through the night.

I hardly seemed to have slept when Cameron was shaking me awake, 'Come on, wakey wakey. We'll make you some breakfast and then we'll be on our way up that hill!'

Annie stayed in bed as we drank our tea and ate our porridge. 'It is a pity we won't be able to keep in contact, since you don't have email or anything,' I said.

'Don't be daft,' he said, before going over to his jacket and taking out a mobile phone. 'I get email on this. And I can make calls and get them. And I charge it up at the sandwich shop. And we're getting a solar panel put on the roof. We aren't daft, you know.'

Cameron woke Annie just before we left so I could say goodbye. She smiled radiantly as she emerged from sleep and told me to be sure that I visit them again, and with that we left via the back door and joined the steep footpath.

As with the day before, a haze lay over the waters of the Firth of Clyde and the Sound of Bute. The seal had resumed its position on the rock. With Cameron leading the way we climbed up the hillside towards Creag Ghlas Laggan before going right towards Cuithe. We carried on uphill along a pathway overgrown with bracken, and the horse flies kept on biting.

Cameron had insisted that we walk in silence for fear of

scaring away the wildlife. As we approached the top of the hillside through bracken we almost walked right into a herd of red deer. They bounded off away from us before stopping to look back. I thought of them suffering with the horse flies.

As we continued across the broad sweep of the hillside, several different groups of red deer retreated before looking back towards us through swaying stretches of cotton grass. The antlers of a stag were profiled against the sea.

After staring at all the herds of deer I looked beyond them at my surroundings. On the one side, seemingly quite close, there was the profile of hills that Cameron said was known as the Sleeping Warrior, and on the other, glimpsed in the distance between swathes of cloud, the Paps of Jura, glistening silver in the sun.

By the time I looked around again, Cameron was in the distance, waving calmly before smiling and then turning to disappear from view. As a gentle bark from a stag broke the silence I stood between the Sleeping Warrior and the Paps of Jura, gazing at the scene.

Then I realised I was slowly sinking into sphagnum moss. And the horse flies had returned. With a jolt I lifted my sinking legs and carried on across the hillside towards Glen Chalmadale, Torr Nead an Eoin standing sentinel above the road from Sannox to Lochranza.

Descending quickly I continued along a cart track behind the backs of houses in Lochranza, skirted around the golf course and came close again to the bay, where the black and white birds, which I now knew to be oystercatchers, were out-numbered by gulls. I thought of Fairy Dell, of Cameron and Annie, and of what Cameron had said about James Hutton's unconformity, and how different it all was from Manchester.

I camped at Lochranza that night and got the bus back to Lamlash in the morning. I rested up for a day, just lounging around the campsite. I was a little nervous of going into the mountains on my own, but Cameron had assured me that in good weather there would be no problem. I looked at the route on the map over and over, getting it clear in my mind.

I got the bus into Brodick. Then I got on the 324 to Lochranza, all the time looking up at the granite bulk of Goatfell rising high in the sunlight above Brodick Bay. I got off the bus just beyond the school, and took the turn down the road towards Glen Rosa. After calling in at the farm I wandered past the white-painted toilet block filled with nesting swallows and found myself a spot on the campsite by Glen Rosa Water.

In the morning I zipped the tent door closed and then wandered down the well-marked track. After the footbridge I took a sharp turn left and made my way uphill beside waterfalls. Soon enough I was high enough to look back down on Glen Rosa, where Glen Rosa Water curved on its descent to the sea at Brodick. There was an anchored tanker in Brodick Bay, and Holy Isle beyond it in the Firth of Clyde.

I followed the waterfalls higher on a path between heather. I saw a hovering kestrel. Beyond the deer fence at the Garbh Allt I climbed gradually higher along boggy ground that gave beneath my feet. To my left the waterfalls were gushing. I looked up at the route of the climb to where mist rose up the face of the mountain. The mist continued to move in, covering and then revealing glimpses of the silver passage of Glen Iorsa as I laboured towards the summit of Beinn Nuis. There was the brief glimpse of a peregrine falcon.

Sitting on a rock by the side of the path I waited for the

mist to clear. Then I realised that it wouldn't clear any time soon. I thought of turning back, but then looked carefully at the map, remembering the route Cameron had shown me. The mist surrounded me, but there was no wind. I sat in the absolute silence with just the mist drifting over the rocks. When my bare legs started to feel cold I moved slowly higher and the stiffness in my knee was painful. I smiled to myself in surprise when I reached the summit cairn in a matter of minutes. A little brown bird sat on the pile of rocks and stones.

On the ridge I looked back at the clear brown path that seemed to lead straight into the waters of Brodick Bay. I looked down between rocks and considered the chasms. I began my slow descent down the slippery grass and moss. Before beginning the rise up towards the summit of Beinn Tarsuinn, I saw a distinctive rock to my right. There were three slabs lying one on top of the other, and the middle one protruded like a nose. This was what Cameron had called the Old Man of Tarsuinn.

I looked carefully at the map again. Then from Beinn Tarsuinn I went down to the Meadow Slabs beside Consolation Tor and sat down to rest. I ate my sandwiches and threw the crusts onto one of the slabs alongside me.

I headed past the Meadow Face and Ealta Choire and then for the first time heard the croaking calls of ravens, turning to see three of them flying around the Meadow Slabs. I reached into my pocket for the packet of Arran oatcakes, breaking off some pieces to eat and placing other pieces on rocks. I could hear the ravens behind me as I made my way to Cnoc Breac.

I hadn't seen anyone all day. I continued the descent and then, as I looked down across the great distances that lead across the damp moorland and the waterfalls, one of the ravens swept in a wide arc before me. It croaked calmly. Another of the ravens appeared and seemed to dive-bomb the other, and then a third raven came, and it seemed they were just playing in the updraughts.

Tired from the walking I continued on the descent. It had been more than enough for me, the kestrel and the waterfalls and the heather and the lochs and the glens and the peregrine falcon and the rock face and the ravens. Then I saw something huge in the sky. I watched the effortless flight and almost immediately tried to discount it. Somehow it looked black. I had never seen anything so big before in my life, or anything flying so effortlessly. When it flew closer I could see that it was not black but dark brown. It was a golden eagle, the most amazing thing I had ever seen.

The next morning was dull and cloudy. I boarded the 8.20 ferry to Ardrossan feeling gutted at having to leave. I went to the cafe and got myself a cup of tea, exchanging pleasantries with the blank-faced woman behind the counter. Behind me in the quickly formed queue a woman and the man with her seemed to recognise my Manchester accent. The woman was dressed in a way that suggested she'd just come out of a nightclub; she wore a long yellow dress and was heavily made up. Her blonde hair wasn't natural. She had the hard eyes of a hooker, and those eyes knifed into me. The man with her had a tattoo reaching up his neck. It seemed I was home already. Both of them seemed to be watching me so I finished my tea and went to sit at the other end of the boat.

As the mountains of the island got smaller I closed my eyes. When I opened them the woman in the yellow dress and the man with the tattoo on his neck were sitting opposite.

They looked at me just long enough after I opened my eyes for me to realise. They smirked at each other and started to kiss. The passengers sitting near them looked away as the two of them grabbed and groped. The man with the tattoo on his neck reached into the yellow dress and fondled her tits. The woman slapped him and adjusted her bra and pretended to be pissed off for about two minutes before they started kissing again. When they stopped for air they both looked over at me and smirked before snogging and groping some more. She put her hand on his crotch. Other passengers got up and moved away.

'Enjoying the view?' said the woman.

'What?' I said.

'Whereabouts in Manchester do you live?' said the man.

'What?'

'Whereabouts?' he said.

'We're from Salford,' she said.

'Small world.'

'What did you go to Arran for?'

'Just went camping.'

'You don't look camp,' he said, laughing stupidly.

'Shut up, Deano.'

'You shut up, Tanya, or you'll get a slap.'

At that she kissed him hard on the lips. 'I can't wait until I get you home.'

'Here, mate. Have you got a spare cig I can borrow?' he said.

'Don't smoke, chief.'

At that they got up from their seats and sat down next to me, Tanya crossing her long shiny legs.

'You won't believe the problems we've had. Tanya's sister

lives in Brodick. Tell us about your trip anyway. Where have you been camping?'

'Lochranza.'

'Lochranza. That where they've got the castle? '

'Yes.'

'And you can get the ferry to Kintyre from there, can't you?' said Tanya.

'Not sure.'

'Can you spare us some change?' said Deano.

'Err . . . I'm a bit skint myself.'

'How you getting back to Manc then?'

'I've got my train ticket.'

'Come on, mate, you must have some spare change for a brew.'

'I can't, sorry.'

'Fuck me, us Mancs should stick together.'

'Sorry, chief,' I said.

'I'm not your fucking chief. Come on, Tanya, let's go and sit somewhere else,' he said, gripping her by the arm. Unfolding her long legs she stood up and tottered off on the high heels. The yellow dress bunched up as Deano gripped her arse.

I got off the ferry and felt Deano and Tanya following me down the covered walkway to the train station. As I waited on the platform in the light rain they stood right near me and then made a show of moving away again.

On the train they walked past and carried on to sit in another carriage. As the train left Saltcoats, Deano passed to go to the toilet, smirking on his way there and on his way back. I imagined him dragging his knuckles on a monkey walk down the aisle. This man must have been about forty and yet he wore his jeans hanging off his arse like a teenager.

The train passed through Stevenston, Kilwinning and Dalry. A man got off at Milliken Park and walked straight into the bushes for a piss. Several young men sat on the platform of Paisley Gilmour holding carrier bags filled with beer cans. It seemed everyone I saw had a tattoo. All the children were trying to look like adults, girls of ten or eleven in crop tops and hot pants and wearing gold earrings and necklaces. I saw one girl smoking and the cigarette looked huge.

At Glasgow Central I looked up at the departure boards and realised I'd have to get a train to Preston and then change again for Manchester. There was work going on somewhere along the West Coast mainline.

On the train to Preston I sat looking out of the window. A Jewish man with a skull cap and headphones on sat opposite me, tapping his feet. I smiled at the sight of it. I put my own headphones on. All week I'd been listening to the Springsteen song 'The Wrestler'. It was on a soundtrack to a film starring Mickey Rourke and I loved both the film and the song. All the way through you see how this old wrestler's life is a pile of a shit and you hope he'll learn from his mistakes. But at the end of the film he just goes back to the way he has always lived. And then Springsteen comes in over the credits. Listening to the song all week, among the beauty of Arran, I had promised myself that I wasn't going to end up like that.

As the train left Carlisle, I was pissed off to see Deano's monkey walk pass me down the aisle. Again there was the familiar smirk, only this time he stopped and rubbed his crotch in front of me. Then he crouched down and put his face right opposite. When he smiled there was silver glinting from his teeth. 'What goes around comes around,' he whispered.

For the first time I began to feel a bit scared of him. As the train sped through Shap, I barely noticed the Lake District mountains. At Preston I got off the train and walked over to platform three, and Deano and Tanya were there, right behind me, getting on at the same door but again sitting in a different carriage.

As I sat by the window I put my hand on my knee and tried to massage some of the pain away. By Preston I had hardly been able to walk at all. A few more knuckle-draggers got on at Chorley, including a topless man smeared in baby oil. And many more people got on the train at Bolton, so that the seats of the carriages filled up and people had to pack the aisles.

When they got off at Salford Crescent, Tanya sneered at me and Deano ran over to bang on the window as the train pulled away. Welcome home. The train continued through Deansgate station and I began to relax a bit as it slowed into Oxford Road. I went out through the barriers and down the steep steps past the Salisbury, then up the cobbled slope. I crossed Oxford Road and went into the tiny newsagents perched above the trickling Medlock and got myself some chewing gum.

Now they'd knocked down the BBC building on Oxford Road I could see my flats. I chewed my gum and stared at the low clouds covering the building. The balcony was lost in mist. That balcony was the only thing I liked about my flat. In the evenings I'd stand out there watching the crows on the roof of the Manchester International College. Once, hot air balloons appeared in the sky. They were red, yellow and green. I heard the gentle whoosh of the flames that kept them in the air but otherwise they were silent as they floated above the Mancunian Way.

I walked down Charles Street and turned right down Upper Brook Street and past the Ibis Hotel. The road was busy but I skipped across between cars and walked below the Mancunian Way, following the pedestrianised route and going under the exit slip. I walked past where I'd been mugged and followed the path around the railings. I went through the car park and put the fob to the door. I went up in the little lift. There was a bloodstain on the floor. I got out and saw foil and needles on the stairwell. There was a man in a sleeping bag lying motionless. I went the length of the walkway and looked back towards the stairwell as I put my key in the lock of the door.

I went out onto the balcony and leant on the rails. The traffic was still busy on the Mancunian Way, rushing in both directions. I went back in and closed my balcony door. I fidgeted around on the couch, irritated by *The X Factor*. Everyone was 'taking the positive'. Such bullshit. I remembered the souvenir mug and fished into my rucksack to look at it. It showed Goatfell above Brodick Bay.

A week or so after the Arran trip I looked through my bookshelves. I picked out all the brand-new books, the ones I'd read but didn't really feel anything for, the clever ones written from the head and not the heart. I put them all in piles on the lino floor. I got a couple of carrier bags and filled them with the books. On the Saturday I took the two carrier bags' worth of new books back into work and put them behind the counter. After putting my jacket in the staff room I came back down and put all the books back on the shelves. Then at lunchtime I went home and brought back two more carrier bags full of new books. I kept the Kerouac and the Steinbeck, and the John Fante ones with glossy covers published by Rebel Inc.

What I didn't know was that they had started to use the CCTV. It was all there on screen. How fucking stupid was I? I thought they might get the police involved and that they would search my flat and take all my books. But they didn't do that, they just sacked me. They knew a load of staff were nicking books from the shop. But they couldn't sack everyone so they made me the scapegoat.

A few weeks later I decided to save money on bus fare by walking to the dole office in Fallowfield. The students had gone home and there were fewer buses running and fewer people standing around waiting for them. I enjoyed the brief sunlight on Oxford Road, shining on the umbrellas stuck in the trees of Whitworth Park as part of an exhibition at the nearby gallery. I walked in through the doors of the dole office. Dead eyes surrounded me, sad people shuffling around and staring at anyone who dared to smile. The moment I stepped in there my spirit began to drain away.

The people working behind the counter all had wired eyes. The men had bad skin and hadn't bothered to shave. The white of their shirts was dull and sweat leaked from under the arms. The women were overweight and wore too much make up. They were all dressed in black. A security guard kept looking at me. When it was my turn I waited by the cordoned-off area until a man with a pronounced hunchback scowled over at me without making eye contact. I sat down and still there was no eye contact.

'What kind of job are you looking for?'
'Anything local really.'
'You can't limit yourself to that.'
'Anything then.'

He sighed and got up and shuffled over to a computer that printed a load of jobs out. 'Okay. There's a call centre one, Post Office temporary job, cleaner in Moss Side.'

'Okay, thanks, I'll have a look.'

I got up and still there was no eye contact. I walked out past the staring security guard and back out into the street. I felt like going straight to an off licence, buying some cans of strong lager and getting shitfaced.

But walking past the Ford Madox Brown I paused and put the paperwork about the jobs into a litter bin. I wouldn't have to go through that misery for another fortnight and this realisation lifted the weight from my shoulders. My rent was being paid and I had a small amount of money for food. I had managed to avoid getting a shit job. On my way home I went to Samir's and put a fiver on the meter card by way of celebration.

The electricity meter was in a cupboard in the kitchen. I put the topped-up card back in and the meter made a strange rattling sound. The fiver didn't seem to register. I realised over the next few days that something was broken. I had hot water all the time but no heating.

There was an armchair left outside the flats. It looked okay and smelled fine. I struggled to get it into the lift but managed in the end. Then I dragged it along the walkway and in through my front door. I put it beside the bookshelf. Looking at all the unread books I realised there was a lot of catching up to do. I made my way through them from left to right, and whenever I felt cold I got up from the armchair and went for a bath.

PART THREE

ASH FELL FROM the sky. The mid-afternoon traffic moved back and forth on the Mancunian Way. Students walked up and down. A tall tree had blown over. A football rolled around on the roof of the Manchester International College. There was another tall building beside the Beetham Tower. Cranes filled the skyline. The woman above dropped more fag ash from her balcony. I went back inside and turned on the IPL cricket. I drifted in and out of sleep until five when I got off the couch and made my tea. It was a Friday evening. After tea I went out for four cans of Carlsberg from Samir's next to the Deaf Institute. On my way back, I looked through the windows of the gym at all the students sprinting on the treadmills. I crossed the road and headed back to Lamport Court. Back in the flat I put three of the cans in the fridge and took the other one out onto the balcony. I also took a notepad and pen, and a copy of *The Days Run Away Like Wild Horses Over the Hills*. I drank the can and read the poems. Soon my own poems came. I followed this technique through the four cans of Carlsberg until my writing became illegible and the light began to fade. I watched the pages of the notepad flapping in the breeze. A crow called from the rooftop of the college. The sign on the Palace Hotel shone brightly.

They called me the next day. I would be working on a Saturday, Sunday and Monday. The first weekend I realised that there was just the woman on the desk and me on my own working upstairs, shelving all the books that those working in the week had left behind. I went to the American Literature section and started reading *The Road to Los Angeles*, and when Angela from the enquiry desk came upstairs I pretended I was putting the book on the shelf. After that I walked back to the trolley with all the other books.

'How is it going?' she asked.

'Seems okay so far.'

'Okay, well, any problems let me know. I have to stay on the desk down there but I'll be up to check on you now and again.'

'Right.'

She went back downstairs and I walked into the PC suite and logged in. I had a look on the BBC sport website and watched a maximum break by Ronnie O'Sullivan. Students slowly began to filter in. Only the sad ones came to the library on a weekend. At least I was getting paid.

At lunchtime I walked through the PC suite and down the back stairs to the staff room. I ate my sandwiches and stole a yoghurt from the fridge. Then I had a lie down on the couch for about half an hour. After that I went back upstairs into the PC suite and waded through the banalities of Facebook. At four I went to the trolley bay and looked at all the trolleys with all the books. I'd emptied one trolley on to the shelves in the morning and now I did another one.

At a quarter to five there was an announcement that the library would be closing in fifteen minutes. Little Pete the porter came up the stairs and started turning off the PCs in the PC suite. He walked around the library asking students to leave. When the last of them had cleared out I turned off the lights and went downstairs to my locker. I put my rucksack on my back and wheeled my bike out of the back door and cycled down Chapel Street through town and back to the high-rise.

On Monday there were all the staff in the offices and loads more people on the enquiry desks and a few other shelvers. And there were students all over the place. I couldn't spend all day on the internet and it was trickier to read. But I kept rereading a Richard Brautigan story about a kid who goes fishing in Oregon.

I was still knackered from cycling the day before so I'd got the train from Oxford Road to Salford Crescent. Dom and Craig, the two other shelvers, asked me if I fancied a pint in The Crescent.

A mouse ran out from under the piano. Two men leaned on the bar. The landlord's jaw was covered in bum fluff. They were giving away free chip butties but the offer wasn't getting students in. Little Pete the porter turned up. He lived just around the corner near the Adelphi campus. I thought he might join us but he stayed at the bar. I looked out of the window at the traffic hurtling by on Chapel Street. Dom was waffling on. 'Worse jobs than this one,' he said. 'I'm fifty though. Too late for me to get anything else.'

I went for a slash. The urinals were light-blue porcelain and stank like a thousand years of piss. Two men came and went without washing their hands. I walked back out of the bogs. There were a few students sitting on the old armchairs below the window. They looked like they were into heavy metal. The three lads took it in turns to talk about themselves to a girl glad of the attention.

'Fancy a wander down to the King's Arms after this?' said Dom, when I sat back down.

'Why not?'

We wandered down Chapel Street. The evening sunlight shone on the walls of the old hospital.

In the King's Arms there were posters on the walls and flyers on the tables advertising gigs and plays and poetry readings in the function room upstairs. On Tuesdays there was a knitting class for the stressed. There were lovely leather seats. On the shelves high on the wall there were piles of old radios. The bar staff were two bearded blokes from a locally famous band. It was my round. I stood there at the bar and they kept talking to each other. A blonde came in and they went over to her.

'Three Guinness,' I said, when one of them came back.

'Pints?'

'Yep.'

Our table was filled with empties, and when the one with the black beard came over I looked at his shoes. They were like jester's boots. I trod on the ends of them but his toes weren't there.

We drank and waffled on for hours.

'Five is my limit,' said Craig.

'Oh come on, Craig,' said Dom.

'I'll be making my way back. Are you walking back that way, Dom?'

'I am.'

I stayed for another after they left. I didn't like Craig. Something about him didn't fit. But Dom was salt of the earth. Listening to him got me through many shifts. I always got on with older blokes. He had thinning grey hair and very bad skin. There were always little shaving nicks on his face and it was obvious he used cheap razors. He came in every day with cheese sandwiches in a carrier bag. He wore blue plastic gloves that made his hands clammy. He wore them because he said the books were full of germs and people coughed on the open pages.

He was an open book. Almost like a child in his honesty.

He lived with his parents all his life. Watched each of them grow old. Lived in the same house after they'd gone. He was self-educated and could talk with authority on all topics except women, who he admitted were a mystery. He made the occasional quip about them always being after his money. He said an ex of his was always putting pictures of herself and her husband on Facebook just to piss him off.

He told me once that he didn't like going to the toilet in the middle of the night and so kept an empty bottle by the bed. With the lid cut off. He loved the music of Al Stewart, said he was the greatest singer songwriter this country had ever produced. He was a tight bastard. Once I borrowed 10p off him because I didn't have enough for a can of Coke. The next day he came up to me straightaway and asked me for it back. I'd forgotten about it and said I'd bring it in next time. I thought he was going to burst into tears.

He talked about himself all the time but wasn't boring. He lived in Swinton, always had. He'd taken a load of drugs in the 60s, said that he and his mates had once run all the way down the side of Ben Nevis. He'd worked in a pharmaceutical place after that and nicked drugs from there. He'd worked as a lab assistant in schools, brought the bulls' eyeballs in for the kids to cut up. Cleaned them all away after. He was by far the hardest worker and the library was his life. On his days off he came in and took science books to a desk and sat there on his own doing experiments. He said that when he retired he wanted to live in a house with a view of the sea, but knew it would never happen.

It was still light outside. I walked past Salford Central. My face was glowing pleasantly. I looked from Bridge Street at a broad stretch of the Irwell. There were swans down there.

I stopped for a pint in the Bridge Street Tavern, sitting by the window and looking at the view of Granada Cleaners. The pub was almost empty. The streets were silent. There were hardly any cars. I had another pint in the Town Hall Tavern. I counted five single men in there, all drinking pints of bitter and reading copies of the *Manchester Evening News*. The buxom barmaid looked suicidal. I wandered down the steps and sat at the back of the pub looking out onto Bow Lane. I wandered over to Albert Square, sat on a bench and looked up at the sunlit clock tower, hoping to see peregrine falcons. I wandered past Manchester Art Gallery and down Princess Street. The brick walls of the Old Monkey, the Circus Tavern and the Grey Horse smelled of ale. I turned right onto Portland Street and headed into the Fab Cafe. There were daleks in the corner and all sorts of shit from TV and the movies on the walls. There was a DJ on. She had been an actress in Coronation Street. Every twenty minutes she left the decks and went outside to smoke. She came from Audenshaw. I fancied her but couldn't be arsed. I had a final Guinness and a last slash. It was dark by now. I headed towards Brook Street and made my way back to the high-rise. I looked up at all the windows but there were no faces there. A dog was tied up on a balcony but it didn't bark.

The next day I wandered back down Princess Street and had a look in the art gallery. It must have been the holidays because it was filled with screaming kids. I wandered around in a daze. I preferred the landscapes to anything else. I walked into a room of sculptures and turned back around again. I walked into a dark room showing a film and fell asleep. In another room there was a small painting by William Blake hidden to one side. I turned the corner and there was a massive canvas there. It was a dead lion. I was staggered. The painting was magnificent and I couldn't get it out of my mind.

On my way back into the flat I got talking to one of my neighbours on the seventh floor. Jake's flat was right by the stairwell and the lift, and he was leaning on the rail and looking across at the view that stretched across to the Etihad Stadium.

'Not working today?' he said to me.

'No. You?'

'Was working on that hotel over there,' he said, pointing to what used to be the BT building on London Road. 'I work when they call me.'

'Agency, is it?'

'Hod carrier.'

'That's hard graft.'

'You're right. Come in for a brew if you want.'

'Nah, mate, you're alright. I'm a bit knackered.'

'If you want to get fucked let me know.'

'What do you mean by that?'

'I mean I can sort you out.'

'Nah, mate, you're okay. Can't afford it these days.'

'You can get a blowjob for a fiver.'

'That's cheap.'

'Yeah. She's got no idea. If you want, next time, after she's been here I'll send her over.'

'Don't like the sound of that, to be honest.'

'Suit yourself.'

One night I came home pissed and had a vague memory of talking to a hooker outside. She followed me into the flats and watched from the other end of the walkway as I fumbled with my keys. The next night I was lying in bed when I was woken by a banging on the front door. I got up and went to look through the spyhole. There were two drunk hookers staggering around there and laughing, their faces like bloated gargoyles.

Two new shelvers started at the library. Sara and Sam were both students. Both had loads of tattoos. Both were always late and took loads of sick leave. Sam in particular had a way of making this seem both inevitable and someone else's fault. Sara was more down to earth, just said it as it was. She took a week off on the sick and nobody said anything, so she just kept taking time off. When they did actually come into work they both made a great performance out of making it seem they were grafters. They kept going for drinks of water, wiping their brows, stretching their backs. I liked them a lot.

Sara worked part time on a pirate radio station in Moss Side. She was well into black culture and told me about a nightclub called the Park, right opposite my flat. We went out for Sara's birthday and she made a great effort to stay sober. She smoked these brown fags from France. I stayed the night in the house she shared with a load of druggies near the old swimming baths in Withington. I was glad of being able to sleep somewhere else. She grunted at me as I left in the morning. On my way out I looked in the living room and there was a guy and a girl zonked out on the couch. The front door was swinging open in the wind. It looked like they'd been robbed.

I walked down Yew Tree Lane down towards Platt Lane. I watched the 111 bus pass me by. I looked at the pitches through the fences. The pitches were perfect. I thought of the hours of practice there, the long evenings in winter and summer. I walked up to Platt Fields. I saw a heron on an island in the middle of the lake. I walked back through the park towards Moss Side, and approached where the stadium used to be. There was a housing development there. There was row after row of flimsy houses that wouldn't last twenty years. The old stadium had stood tall for a century. I walked around to the chippy on Claremont Road. It didn't open until twelve. The streets were filled with all kinds of crap blowing in the wind: chip trays, newspapers, fag packets, Coke cans, crisp packets, cardboard boxes. There were broken couches and three-legged tables, wheelie bins blown over, a pile of mountain bikes with flat tyres. I looked up at the side of an old terraced house. The street sign, 'Maine Road', was still there. I walked past a betting shop and three West Indian blokes leaned on the window outside, smoking cigarettes. There were Somalis, Polish, women in hijabs, men and women of nationalities I could only guess at. There was an upturned wheelie bin on Fred Tilson Close.

I walked through Whitworth Park. The gallery was closed for refurbishment. I sat on a bench in the morning sunlight. I thought of the Springsteen song, 'Wrecking Ball.' It was about the demolition of Giants Stadium in New Jersey. They had done the same to Maine Road. But the Etihad Stadium was magnificent and the new houses on the site of Maine Road were needed. I just wished that the people didn't leave so much shit blowing across the ground. And I wished the building contractors would come back and finish the job off properly, have some respect for what they'd built. From what I could see, there was more than just the stadium that had been destroyed by the wrecking ball.

Sara and Sam milked the shelving job for as long as they could and then they left, Sara moving back to London after her MA and Sam jacking in her degree and heading to Kerala with her boyfriend.

Working with Sara and Sam was the first time I had ever worked alongside women. At primary school we were segregated from the girls by a brick wall in the playground. I went to an all-boys secondary school, played football for years and then worked in a warehouse. Talking in a natural way helped me in my understanding of women. There was nothing to be nervous about.

Sara and Sam were replaced by two men in their fifties: Billy, who'd done thirty years at Clayton Aniline, and Michael, a miserable fucker. Both of them were slower at shelving than Sara and Sam had been, but they were never late and they turned up every day. Billy was a United fan and he told me once that when United won the league they filled the canal near Clayton Aniline with red dye. He also said they made explosives there during the war. I got on with Billy pretty well until he made a casual joke about twatting his wife because she wouldn't shut up. I never got a word out of Michael for a long time but when I did it was pretty funny. The two of them were always chatting with Dom.

One day, Dom was standing in the trolley bay. As usual we were pissing in the wind trying to get all the books on the shelves, and there were about a dozen trolleys there, filled with books. He was putting each trolley full of books into number order, so it could be quicker for everyone else to shelve. At first I thought this was typical of Dom, working hard to benefit others. But maybe he found that easier than shelving.

'This is a joke,' he said. 'How can they expect us to keep on top of all this? First of all they employ two girls who could barely lift a book between them. I mean they were nice girls,

I know, and I don't mean to say anything bad about them but come on. And now Billy and Mike, well. And as for those people on the enquiry desks downstairs. You know there was a time when they put the books in number order down there, and then when we brought them up all we had to do was shelve them. Then that Angela got in on the act and they said they needed people free to deal with student enquiries. I mean, they don't even stamp the books any more. Students just come in and throw them in the book bins. And we are the ones who have to go down and empty the bins, fill the trolleys, wheel the trolleys into the lift, wheel them over into this corner, put them all in order and put them all on the shelves and deal with student enquiries because there's no enquiry desk on this floor. There was a time when we just had to shelve the books. We do all this extra stuff now and we're on the same money as always. It's a joke really.'

'I guess I'm not used to anything else.'

'Oh well, I suppose it's not so bad. At my age I can't be doing anything else.'

The next day there was the monthly shelvers meeting. It was chaired by Ron, a hyperactive man who worked on the enquiry desk and gave the role too much importance. These meetings were just a part of some all-for-one, one-for-all management bollocks in which every member of staff had the same amount of meetings and was treated equally. They said this but the other staff looked at us like we were dipped in shit. Ron rushed in and we were sitting there in one of the private-hire rooms waiting. His bald head was sweating. It was the old routine: the longer we kept him talking the longer we could just sit there. Dom worked full time in this job and he really did more than anyone else. These meetings were the chance for him to say the same things he'd said to me. Ron asked, 'Is there anything else, are there any issues we haven't covered?' and I looked at Dom. We all looked at Dom. He looked down at the desk and fiddled with his hands. The poor bastard was scared of rocking the boat. I didn't say anything. For me the job was a piece of piss. It paid the rent and gave me time to write, and I wasn't really arsed about anything else. But I hated to see Dom act like that.

After the shelvers meeting we went back up to the first floor. I ended up shelving some books in the same aisle as Billy. 'Why didn't he fucking say anything? He's always fucking moaning to us. No wonder the fucking unions have gone to shit,' he said.

There was a loud 'Shsssssh!' from a student so we walked a few aisles down. 'Like I was saying. We wouldn't have put up with this shit at Clayton Aniline. We had our own fucking canteen there and woe betide anyone else came in there. He's got no balls.'

'Why didn't you say anything then?'

'Well, more than my job's worth, isn't it? And anyway the thing is we're all part time, he does this every week. They take advantage of him.'

'He's a grafter, that's for sure.'

'It's whatever gets you through the day, isn't it? He likes to keep busy and when he's not busy he's talking. I tell you something though, he's a tight sod. Never gets a round in. We were in the Crescent on Friday and I got them in and then Mike got them in, and when it was Dom's round he starts umming and ahhing and says he has to go, he'll get the first round next time. That's what he said the time before.'

'Shhhhhhhhhsh!'

'Oh for fuck's . . . can't talk in this place. I'm going for my break anyway. I'll see you later, cock.'

'No probs.'

There had been heavy rain and wind. The water funnelled in through the side of the high-rise and leaked from the ceiling, dripping onto the lino. I put the light on in the living room. There was a pathway through the dust to the couch. I went into the bathroom, looked at the bags under my eyes and rubbed at my itchy beard.

The heating in my flat was still broken, so I sometimes sat in the Central Library for warmth. One day I'd been on a computer and sat there looking up at the beautiful ceiling. Two policemen came in and grabbed me by the arms and frogmarched me out. Someone in the library had had their phone stolen. I'd been on the computer next to them. I hadn't logged off properly and my name was still on the computer. Someone on the library staff had told the police. They took me in for questioning at Bootle Street. I kept telling them I hadn't done it but everyone says that. I told them I'd been on the books at City. Finally it dawned on them that having a beard and a walking jacket didn't automatically make me a scally.

On my way home I sat in St Peter's Square. Cameras twitched high above. An old man smoked a cigarette. Two council workers kept a low profile on the other side of the square. When the old man crushed the cigarette with his foot they gave him a £70 fine. When others came along for a smoke I pointed out the council workers. One of the council workers came over to me and asked if I was going to follow them to Piccadilly Gardens. I said I might.

I liked Monday nights the best, when everyone was

recovering from the weekend and all the streets were quiet. I went in the Town Hall Tavern, Night and Day, the Sandbar, the Fab Cafe, the Roadhouse, the Ruby Lounge and dozens of others I can't remember. I would drink Guinness and stand at the bar. There was a place called the Temple of Convenience. It was a converted shithole.

One time I met the actor Christopher Eccleston. He seemed like a nice bloke. The bar was called Tmesis and it was right next to Cellar Vie. There was some really weird live music. Men with moustaches bashing bathtubs with baseball bats and drilling holes in wood as Japanese girls played triangles and cow bells. I finished my pint and got the hell out of there.

On Lever Street a man was taking a woman from behind. I kept walking. I ended up in Ancoats. The tram stop there was called New Islington.

I looked in through a window and saw hordes in a brightly lit room watching a man with a gas mask. Another mad muso. The men all had beards and the women all wore bright-red lipstick and polka-dot dresses. I'd never seen so many daft hats in one place.

I had a few scoops with Jammo in Cellar Vie. He said that it stayed open as a nightclub and loads of fit black women would be coming in later. I'd been in there before with Scoie and never realised it was a club. The lager was dirt cheap and we had plenty of it. Jammo had a kip on the table at one point. Late on the women started to filter in. Most people in there were black. Then something miraculous happened: all the women moved onto the dance floor and started shaking their booty. The lad behind the bar smiled at me and said it was called 'bogling'. The women were dancing as much for themselves as for the men standing goggle-eyed by the dance floor. I had never seen anything like it. I didn't know where to look. All the other men were just openly staring. And then a guy walked up to this girl and rubbed up and down against her backside with his cock.

There was one woman there at the edge of a group of her friends. She shook her booty quite demurely compared to them, looked a little shy. Me and Jammo went home with a couple of white birds to their flat in Whalley Range but it was the shy girl I remembered.

I saw her again in Manchester Art Gallery a few weeks later. I shuffled around in front of the lion painting, and she was there in the reflection of the glass that covered the canvas.

'You go in Cellar Vie, don't you?' I said.

'Err . . . yes, I do.'

'I was in there a few weeks back. Lively place.'

'Yes it is,' she said.

'I love this lion one.'

'Me too. So sad.'

'Have you got time for a coffee?'

'Err . . . I suppose so, though I have to be back in work soon.'

'Where do you work?'

'Just in the bank.'

'Which one?'

'TSB on Cross Street.'

We went into the café and she found us a table by the window. I came back with the coffees on a tray. There was something about her.

She told me her name – Denise – and gave me her phone number and we exchanged texts for a while, then longer emails. I met her for a drink in Cellar Vie and we went back to hers. She had a nice flat in Whalley Range. She had the Friday off during the week and so I went round to hers on a Thursday night. We sat on her couch kissing for hours on end. My neck got stiff. I loved the kissing but my balls were aching.

I offered to sleep on the couch and so she brought me a duvet. In the night I could hear that she was still awake so I got up and wandered into her bedroom. 'We don't have to do anything,' I said.

She pulled back the covers. I climbed in and soon we started kissing. Then I moved inside her gently. Her whole body was burning hot. It was the first time I had ever done it sober. Afterwards I fell asleep with my arms around her.

Not long after that she sent me a text telling me that she loved me. And then she kept asking me, 'Do you love me?' At first I said I wasn't sure, because I wasn't, and it pissed her off, made her sulk, caused arguments. So I started telling her that I loved her.

I shaved off my beard and started doing sit-ups. I stopped going to Samir's for beer. I felt more confident than I had in a long time. I was in a couple. There was someone in my corner and I didn't need anything more.

Denise started calling and texting every day. At first it was fine. I tried to tell her not to text me in the mornings. I had to try to write. She took it personally. I couldn't concentrate anyway. The heat of her body was all I could ever think about, and lying against her arse was unbelievable.

But as I walked down the street I started to look at all the women of the city: blondes, brunettes, red heads, short hair, long hair, slim, fat. With the confidence Denise gave me I started to think that I could have them all.

I had to account for every moment I wasn't with Denise, long explanatory conversations that left me feeling knackered. I felt the walls closing in and wanted to head for the hills.

I had another night out with Jammo. We sat having a few quiet pints in the Lass O'Gowrie. Denise kept texting me over and over and I was sick of it. I couldn't string a sentence together to Jammo without my phone ringing. In the end I just turned it off.

In the morning I rolled gingerly across the bed and turned on my phone. The light from the screen hurt my head. There were dozens of texts and missed calls. I called Denise without reading any of them first and she was ranting at me, telling me how worried she had been. My head was pounding and I told her I didn't love her.

We met a few times after that, but I'd fucked us up. Once was in a little café on Mount Street. I didn't know it then but she was already seeing somebody else. I was looking at her long fingernails when she told me. I asked to get back together and she said that would never happen, and we both had tears in our eyes. I wandered through town and got on a tram. I forgot to get a ticket and when the inspector started to tell me about the fine I said that I'd just split up with my girlfriend, as though it made any difference.

If only she'd given me more space. If only I had been more mature. If only I'd had some experience and known how to deal with it. I tried to contact her, but she'd blocked my email, and when I went round to her flat in Whalley Range she'd moved. Without her all my confidence had gone.

On Sunday morning I looked down on the crescent of the Irwell. I saw a heron by the side of the river's curve. I passed the Maxwell Building and Peel Park and the Cockcroft

Building on my way to the staff entrance at the back of the Clifford Whitworth Library. I waited a few minutes for Little Pete to arrive with the keys and then I followed him in and put my coat and my carrier bag into my locker. I went upstairs and put all the lights and computers on and then logged in myself.

Craig was in his early thirties. On the anniversary of each of his parents' deaths, he came into work wearing black. He would be sulking all through his shift. But then the day after he would be back to his bright self, seemingly happy to go out of his way to help everyone he could. People thought he was a nice guy and everyone was sorry he'd lost his parents. But this one time I was tidying books on the next row along and he didn't notice I was there. Dom walked down that aisle and started talking to him with his usual smile on his face. Craig started on at him about putting books back in the wrong place, prodding him in the chest and being really aggressive. Dom was such a gentle guy and it made me angry to see it. I confronted Craig and he went red in the face.

Over the summer we had to properly tidy the shelves, making sure every book was in its right place and shifting great amounts of stock around in order to accommodate new books. Only Craig took the option of overtime to join me on the Sunday. We'd managed to avoid each other until then.

A laminated piece of card stuck out from the shelves to show where we'd got up to the day before. We stood beside each other, going through the shelves, checking the numbers were all in the right order. We barely exchanged a word. At lunchtime, Craig went outside to smoke while I sat in the staff room eating someone's yoghurt.

After the afternoon break we reached the folio section, the

place where the shelves were wider apart to accommodate the really big books like atlases and collections of photography. I'd climbed onto the top shelf to reach around in the dust and lift off a folio that had been dumped there because it didn't fit in the right place. I'm not sure if I meant to do it or not but somehow the folio fell off the shelf and hit Craig on the head.

He pulled me off the lockers and we pushed and shoved each other, causing the shelves to wobble. He swung a fist at me and hit me on the shoulder and then I punched him on the nose. He ran off to the bathroom to get something to stop the blood. I went down to the ground floor where Angela was reading something on the internet. I put my swipe card to the staff room door. I went to my locker and got my coat and carrier bag and left the building some twenty minutes before the end of the shift. I walked past the Cockcroft Building and Peel Park and then the Maxwell Building. I looked down at the curve of the Irwell and saw the heron in the branches of a tree. I crossed at the traffic lights on Chapel Street and went back towards the Crescent. I went in the pub and got a pint and drank it while standing at the bar.

I called in sick on Monday and all week I waited for a phone call. I went back in on Saturday. Little Pete said nothing. Angela said nothing. I checked my emails, and there it was, a message saying that disciplinary procedures were under way, and that I would be contacted again soon.

Three weeks later I had an email telling me that a disciplinary panel was in the process of being assembled. Three months later, I received an email telling me that I was required to give my own version of events in writing, which I duly did.

The incident might have been captured on CCTV but the

cameras were never switched on. A disciplinary meeting was finally arranged. Those appointed to the panel were completely impartial because none of them had been there.

I read out my statement, and added only that I hoped that everyone could 'finally move on'. I was informed that Craig had not been able to attend because he was still undergoing counselling. I wondered what would happen next, and was told I would be informed in writing of the decision.

Every day I checked my pigeonhole. There was just the glossy magazine. It featured the achievements of staff and photographs of charismatic behaviour at the annual Smiths tribute night at the Crescent. Finally I saw a plain brown A4 envelope there. I wasn't sure about opening it and felt butterflies in my stomach. Was this the end? I took the envelope upstairs and sat on a footstool pretending to tidy the American fiction. *The Road to Los Angeles* was out on loan. I opened the envelope, took out the paperwork, and skipped through the twenty-seven pages to the end.

On the Saturday night I went out and got pissed. I didn't know if I was celebrating or drowning my sorrows. Anyway I still had a job. I ended up in a nightclub on Grosvenor Street called the Park, the one that Sara had told me about. The bouncers took a good look at me and when I got inside I realised I was just about the only white guy in the place. I stood at the bar drinking a can of Red Stripe, and soon enough the black women were bogling. There was a woman there giving it everything. She wore a lot of makeup and had hair extensions and wore the smallest white dress I had ever seen. There was no knicker line. She seemed to dance more manically than anyone else around, and soon enough she was bumping and grinding. This bloke looked older than her. His dancing seemed a bit aggressive, and the woman leered over at me. It was Denise. I walked towards her still holding my can of Red Stripe and the bloke pushed me away. I spilled my beer and nearly fell over.

I wandered outside. A young black lad with glasses cooked chicken on a makeshift barbecue. I bought some off him and sat on the grass outside Lamport Court eating it. It tasted great but a few minutes later I vomited on the grass. I pissed in the lift on the way up, forgetting they had cameras in there. I got a warning letter for that too. In the morning I picked up my old TV, one of those heavy ones from the 90s, and threw it off my balcony. In the afternoon, after a kip, I went down there and cleared it all up, cutting my hand on the broken pieces.

Then to top it all Riggers came back. He must have done his stretch at Strangeways or wherever. He banged on my door in the middle of the night. But when I got out of bed and looked through the spyhole nobody was there. It happened over and over and then one time when I looked he was there, smiling, arm in arm with his blonde hooker girlfriend. From what my neighbour Jake had said about the hooker who sucked his cock for a fiver, I reckoned he had to be talking about her. So now Riggers was back, still short and shaven headed but stockier, and with a daft little goatee beard that made him look like the devil. When he wasn't banging on my door he was whistling up at my windows from outside. Every night my sleep was interrupted. He was trying to drag me down into his sordid pit and I knew I had to get out of the flats.

After coming home pissed one night I started banging on his door. I banged so hard I thought the door might give way. I shouted at him over and over to come out and there was no answer. When I woke the next day I panicked about it and waited for reprisals. For a week there was nothing. And then the whistles started again.

I looked out of the window but I was always too late. And then I saw someone else whistling up at the window. It was an old West Indian in a Panama hat. I liked him. He walked around as though nothing mattered. It couldn't have been him every night. Was I going mad? Didn't these twats realise a whistle would wake others? Why couldn't they use the intercom or their phones? The whistles came on the hour every hour, as they had before. It had to have been Riggers. It was some psychological trick. I didn't know what I could do about it. I started drinking more to sleep through it.

One afternoon I watched from the window as Riggers sat on a wall on Grosvenor Street. I couldn't hear what he said. At first the women smiled and then looked disgusted, and he leered after them, cackling. He had his hands down his pants. He took off his shirt and sat there waiting for more women to walk by. He followed one to her car and put his hand on her opened door to stop her shutting it. She smiled nervously and he let her close it. Then he banged on her window. As rush hour approached the cars built up on Grosvenor Street, backing up from the traffic lights all the way past the college and the Salvation Army. Riggers walked up to women in their cars, and showed them his muscles, and groped himself. He sat on the bonnet of a car. When the woman moved off he shouted, outraged, kicking out at the cars as they passed him.

I could just about pay my rent and survive working three days per week. I read all the novels on my shelves again. I got eBooks dirt cheap and read them on my phone. I went to readings by locally famous writers.

I wasn't interested in any relationships with anyone any more. I just wanted to write and be left alone.

My poems and stories reached into the hundreds and I began sending them off to little magazines. I'd waited long enough before sending them out to know some were bound to find a home. I went to Samir's for stamps. I put stamps on the envelopes and took them down to the postbox on Grosvenor Street. It was months before I got any replies. I preferred the brief 'yes' or 'no' ones. The ones where the editors gave specific reasons for not choosing them just wound me up, and I tossed those into the bin without reading the rest of what they said. One time I sent drafts and redrafts back and forth with an editor only to be rejected in the end. I never did that again. The editors who accepted my poems were angels and when they wrote back I kissed their words. I strode down the street as a published writer. I had no money and I looked like a scally, with my beard re-grown and my tattered walking jacket and my walking shoes caked in crap. To the people at work I was just a part-time shelver who'd twatted a colleague. What did they know? Those mugs worked all their lives in jobs they hated just so they could travel to work in a shiny car and upgrade to the latest smartphones. I was a flâneur, for shit's sake.

The first reading I did after my book of short stories was published was at Manchester Central Library. I sent an email to Denise even though I knew she'd blocked me. I thought maybe she'd find it in the spam. The night before the reading I was so excited, thinking of witty anecdotes with which to entertain the adoring public, before drawing them into the subtleties and lyricism of my nuanced prose. I shared the bill with a flash fiction writer called David Gaffney. The little sod stole the show, justifying his top billing on the posters. I sat at the table next to him, watching as he signed and sold copy after copy to the long line of people waiting for a few seconds of his attention. The big pile of my books remained largely untouched until an old woman bought a copy out of sympathy.

I had hoped so much for Denise. When she didn't turn up the life just drained from me. It all seemed so pointless. The publisher had given me a big pile of postcards with the book cover and details on. Nobody had taken any and after the crowd had gone I watched a woman at the library drop them all into a bin. A few of us went to the Town Hall Tavern where younger writers of Gaffney's acquaintance asserted themselves and damned me with faint praise. I got shit-faced and woke up in the bottom of a phone box.

I was told by my publisher that I had to promote the book. I hated the banality of Facebook. I saw Twitter as pointless. Reading any blog I had always thought, after reading one sentence, who gives a shit? I turned down a reading in the rain on a Sunday afternoon in St Ann's Square in the company of twenty other writers. Another reading I did was in a room above the Salisbury on a Monday night of pissing rain and cold in October. The reading was advertised in the local listings. The poet I was reading with put it on his Facebook page and plugged it on Twitter. We arranged all the chairs into rows and then into a semi circle. We tested the mike and did practice readings. I had planned what to read, even planned my ad-libs, and was determined to put on a show this time. No fucker turned up. I heard the heels of a woman on the stairs. They got halfway up, stopped and went back down. I've always wondered if it was Denise.

I went to readings by other writers, sat on the front row

and sneered at them. I got up halfway through to go to the toilet and came back apologising. It was a standard move among writers. Looking around the audience one time at the Central Library I saw a lot of the same faces that had been at my reading there. At the break and at the end they helped themselves to the free biscuits and coffee.

I read to a sparse audience at the International Anthony Burgess Centre on Cambridge Street. I wasn't a massive fan of Burgess, but I liked *The Piano Players*. He'd fucked off out of Manchester as soon as he could, but at least he was originally from here. He lived on Moss Lane East and above an off licence on Princess Parkway.

It became clear to me that the people who really loved Manchester and banged on about the place and its music heritage and all that bollocks were people who had moved here from somewhere else. It was always people from different places who went on about The Smiths and The Fall. The Smiths drained me of hope and I couldn't listen to The Fall. I'd known enough piss-artists for one lifetime.

I watched young bands from a seat in the Ruby Lounge. The audience made up of their friends and family. Just like readings really. The more friends and family you could get to come to your gigs then the more successful you appeared to be. I didn't tell my parents about it. They had no interest in literature. If I'd have asked them to come they would have, but it would have been a chore for them. At least these would-be rock and rollers got laid. I couldn't stand the self-indulgent ones, noodling away on expensive guitars, but women seemed to love that shit.

One of these young bands would get a good review some-where and people would be queueing around the block to pay twenty quid a time. I paid for my ticket at the bar. When I looked around at the audience most of them were talking or on their phones. The important thing was to be there. What bollocks. These people acted in ways I just didn't understand. They had all the right clothes, read all the latest books, and were into the big-name bands of the moment. This was a culture of conformity in the society of the spectacle. I had read those fuckers. When the bouncers threw me out I walked the dark streets down the back roads and pissed up the walls on my way.

My book was reviewed twice. I read both reviews. The one who praised the book had only read the first couple of stories. The other one was damning. It missed the point but had more depth to it. I contacted BBC Radio, but I was just one of a hundred new writers to them.

I did a reading at Salford University because I worked there. There was a Q&A session with creative writing students after. They kept asking me how to get published. They asked about contracts, money. All the questions were about them, not about my writing. Some came to the Crescent after. I got eighty quid for it and pissed it all up the wall. The book sold about a hundred copies, and my mum and dad bought forty of those.

Riggers was still keeping me awake with his whistling and banging. I bumped into him in the car park. He was with the blonde hooker and what I guessed was the blonde's mum. They'd just got out of a battered old Golf. All of them were drinking cans of lager. I was on my way out and kept walking, but the hooker's mum screamed out after me, 'Who do you think you are? Who the fuck do you think you are?' And then Riggers joined in. 'Come back here and I'll kick your fucking head in!' I smiled back at them, pretending I didn't care.

I didn't want to go back to the flats that night so I stayed out, necking pints in different pubs. I didn't remember getting home. In the morning I realised I hadn't even locked my door. I called Longsight police and said I was being threatened by my neighbour. But the police won't do anything until you actually get knifed.

When I was a kid we called it the tip. Then it became the fields. Scoie called them the paddy fields. I went on there with my mate Houghy, who lived on Oakwood Avenue in Audenshaw. It had to be decent weather though. If it had been pissing down we preferred to play football on the street, using someone's gate for a goal. One time this bloke came out and slapped Houghy on the cheek after he'd run into the garden for the ball. Once we broke a window in the house of the old woman who lived in the end terrace next to my parents. She was called Mrs Bantoft. She was about a hundred years old and had a goitre on her neck. Houghy twatted a screamer over the wall and it cracked a little window in the side of her house. When he went in for the ball she came out and tapped him on the shoulder and he shit himself. She looked like a ghost, all pale and white and slow moving. And that goitre was the stuff of nightmares. Houghy ran onto the fields. In the evening I helped my dad nail a board up over where the window had been. After that Houghy was always trying to break windows with the football. He was a little wild. A few years later he stole my mum's Mini from outside the house. He was also into glue sniffing. They found him with a bag over his head on the astroturf cricket pitch near Poplar Street.

When we were kids we were always pretty similar. We had a race across the fields at primary school and it was a dead heat. We got the same kinds of marks for tests and were both in the top five in class. Some years he was a place ahead of me and vice versa. The devil in him got me into scrapes. We mugged Brownie on the steps of Red Hall Church, egged each other on to steal football stickers from Dombovand's sweet shop, and took turns to piss in the shallow end when we went on the coach to Droylsden baths on a Friday.

At Easter there was the Easter egg competition. He just wrote the names of City players all over his. When it came last he dropped it down the back of a cupboard in the classroom. Eventually it started to stink the place out and Mrs Rushton got the caretaker Mr Bates in to drag out the cupboard and clear it away. One of the first times I went to Maine Road with my dad, Houghy came with us. We went to the usual place halfway up the Kippax near the halfway line and sat on the rails there together. He disappeared at half time and my dad started to worry. Houghy came back with a match programme and that devilish glint in his eye. Dad always said he was a cheeky little bugger.

I bet Riggers had been like Houghy as a kid. He got in with the wrong crowd because that's what he wanted to do. Normal life was too boring for them. Houghy always wanted to do something risky. He got me into garden creeping, what some kids called garden hopping. You started at one end of a street and climbed over all the fences in all the back gardens until you got to the end. People were always coming out of their houses and chasing us over the back fence. I guess it was only a small step from that to nicking stuff from people's gardens and from that to robbing houses.

Houghy was the first person ever to make me think I was good at football, and for that reason I always felt fond of him. He encouraged me to play for Audi Rovers, a new team that was starting in the Tameside League. They were getting beat all the time and then I joined, and a couple of lads from Abbey Hey joined, and suddenly we were winning the league. Then I got picked for Tameside Boys, and it was while playing for them that a scout saw me and invited me to Platt Lane. Houghy was a decent player, but he seemed to know how good I was before I knew it myself. He went around telling everybody. I wish I could have kept in touch with him.

When I see the fields now I think of Houghy and all the times we spent together. We picked blackberries from the railway embankment, dropped stuff onto trains from bridges, tied frogs to the line, snapped all the branches in trees, graffitied our names onto the metal bridge. Under that bridge there was a little place you could stand out of the rain. A bar went across and you could do pull ups on it. We stood there eating chocolate bars we'd nicked from Dombovand's.

One time we were on the fields and a load of workers came out of the factory on Groby Road. They all had blue overalls on and heavy steel toe cap black boots, and they made goals with their jumpers. Houghy asked if we could play with them and we did, him on one side and me on the other, and they gave Houghy a bit of stick when they realised how much better I was. He fouled one of them in revenge, tripping him up so that he fell on his face, and this big factory worker got up and started running after him. But Houghy was always fast. Nobody could ever catch him. Everyone knew he was a naughty lad and a lot of parents didn't want their kids to play with him. But he had a lot of life in him and didn't just do what he was told. I wish he was still around.

On Tuesdays I couldn't be arsed walking to work so I got the train from Oxford Road to Salford Crescent. It was the Windermere train. I always felt like staying on it. Time after time I loitered by the opened doors at Salford Crescent before getting off.

On the second floor in the library there were OS maps and I flicked through them. I worked out a walking route through the Lake District, something I could do in a couple of days. At the end of the day I stuffed the map down my pants and went home.

I got off the train at Windermere and took a bus to Ambleside. From there I walked up to Grisedale Tarn, dropped down into the Grisedale Valley and followed the muddy footpath. There were red kites in the sky. I put up my trusty Coleman Cobra tent at the far end of the campsite at Side Farm in Patterdale. I sat looking at the southern end of Ullswater and then wandered into the village for a pint and something to eat. I walked back in the darkness, helped by the light from a head torch I'd bought from Go Outdoors. In the tent I read *All Quiet on the Orient Express*, chuckling to myself all the while. I slept well and in the morning headed up the hillside towards Angle Tarn. I sat by the still pools, looking across at the clouded summit of Helvellyn and listening to all the tiny birds around me. There were roe deer in the morning sunlight on Satura Crag. I almost walked past them without noticing. I joined up with the course of the old Roman road on High Street, strolling through the sunlight. The grasses sparkled. I walked around on High Raise and found a good site for my tent on Kidsty Pike. I put up the tent and left my gear in there and wandered around near Raven Howe looking at the birds. All day long people charged up and down, banging and scraping their walking sticks on the ground.

By late evening the people had gone from the paths and the light was golden. I could just glimpse Haweswater, and on the other side of the path the deer forest of Martindale. I'd bought a loaf of bread in Patterdale and I brought scraps of crust to drop on the ground. Soon ravens began to come. Floating on the thermals they dropped down and picked up the crusts, maybe thirty yards away from me. When they flew off they rolled and tumbled, and turned in vast circles and snuck up behind me, and then, bright enough to realise there was no more food, rose higher into the sky.

I got in the tent and reluctantly finished the novel. It was the first time I had camped wild. There were no other tents around me, no screaming kids, no muppets with guitars, and best of all it was completely free. I needed to piss. I got up and unzipped the tent doors and stood naked in the darkness. There were red lights on a tower somewhere near Carlisle. The moon made everything silver and I sprayed piss everywhere. When I finished I couldn't hear anything except the breeze flapping the tent.

In the morning the tent walls were bright. I had coffee and porridge before packing up and heading to Pooley Bridge. I got the ferry the length of Ullswater to Glenridding. I camped again at Side Farm in Patterdale and then walked back the way I had come, along the Grisedale valley, turning around every few yards to look back at the red kites in the sky.

For a few days after that I felt better. If only I had asked

Denise for some space everything would have been okay. But the traffic on the Mancunian Way killed me. You couldn't get silence there for love or money. The nights were always filled with shouts and screams and wolf whistles and car horns and slamming doors and breaking glass and sometimes the occasional gunshots. Some twats left their music on all night, and all the time there was the traffic, the endless traffic.

The council came and cut down all the surrounding trees. Something to do with health and safety. The chainsaws lopped off the branches and they cut sections at a time. In the end there were just stumps. I wondered why we didn't just concrete over the whole fucking world and have done with it. I wanted to forget it all: City, Denise, Houghy, dead lions, cut-down trees, everything. I got four cans of Carlsberg from Samir's, drank them quickly and marched out into the night.

I wandered down Oxford Road to a shithole called Big Hands. I sat at the bar with my jacket still on. I sneered at the staff while drinking Guinness and then Jameson's. They always served the pretty people first. I remember landing on the pavement near the Holy Name Church, then someone landing on me. The paperwork said I'd punched a wing mirror. A policeman with a luminous coat and holsters told me to shut up. I said to him that he looked about fucking twelve. He told me to shut up. I told him to fuck off. He threatened to throw me in the back of the van unless I shut up. Again I told him to fuck off. He shoved me into the back of the van. In the cell I shouted and swore and kicked the walls. I shouted about having played for City. I vomited into the toilet. A face at the door asked if I was okay. I said I was cold and they gave me a blanket.

In the morning I was still drunk. The police at the station

were friendly. I was courteous and they were surprised. I went through the fingerprinting and the paperwork and the DNA stuff and chatted to each man in turn. One of them mentioned Longsight. I thought I was at Bootle Street.

In the inside pocket of my coat I had a copy of *A Moveable Feast*. I told them that Hemingway had been to Longsight and had said, 'Longsight stays with you. Because Longsight is a moveable feast.' I put the plastic bag that had held my belongings onto the desk and said thanks. The desk sergeant said, 'We'll see you next time.'

Those words stayed with me. I was no fucking flâneur. I was a part-time shelver, single, living in a council flat, with no car and no money, and no prospects of financial security. I went to my mum and dad's. I didn't tell them about my night in the cell. I had some proper meals and caught up on kip.

Leaving my mum and dad's I walked down Stamford Road and then onto Audenshaw Road. I went past Red Hall Church, a totally new building from the one I'd sung hymns in as a kid, and onto Ash Street, passing Edward Street. The old Dombovand's sweet shop was now just a normal house and nobody except my mum remembers me stealing from there.

Lumb Lane School looked much as I remembered except for the portacabins. The red-brick walls were the same and the single-glazed windows and the green railings were still there. I passed the playing fields and remembered scoring the winning goal in a game we won 3-2. We didn't have goalposts then, just cones. There was some dispute about the height of the free kick I scored but Mr Holmes allowed it because he didn't like Houghy.

It was on that field that I saw Emma Bardsley running in a yellow T-shirt. That began my lifelong obsession with big knockers. Another time I hit some sixes playing cricket and the tennis ball landed on Lumb Lane. Once playing football the ball went over the railings and landed in the back of a lorry and we had to run after it.

When I played for Audi Rovers we changed in the school, where the caretaker, Mr Bates, kept his mops and buckets. The mops had shaggy heads and the buckets were a dull metal that clanked and scraped on the floors. The place smelled of disinfectant, sour milk and old socks.

Out through the school gates we trailed down the avenue. The playground and the unmarked playing field were behind the green rails to our left. We went up the hill and across the railway bridge before clattering down the hill in our boots, grabbing railings on the right to slow us down before going in through the tiny gap in the fence.

The two sets of goalposts leaned above bare patches and puddles in the goalmouths. We opened up the sacks and dragged out the netting and then attached it to the goal posts on the little hooks. Brownie went in net and we took turns to cross for headers and volleys while we waited for Dukinfield Tigers.

I went past Jamie Woodcock's place but instead of carrying on past Ryecroft Library I cut down Slate Lane where Marshy and Dolts lived. Marshy lives in L.A. and is on Facebook. I never see Dolts on there, and the bungalow he lived in that backed onto the canal has long since been demolished. His dad was a strange-looking bloke who used to pick Dolts up in an old black cab. Marshy was an artist even back then. His dad used to run a sweet shop and sometimes we'd raid the stock and feast on liquorice string. Me, Marshy and Dolts used to like playing with model cars. I remember getting the bus to Ashton once and there used to be a grassy mound at the back of the bus station and we sat there. Marshy had bought six little Trans Am cars from Woolworths, all in different colours, and we played with them on the grass.

From Slate Lane I made my way across Manchester Road and then cut through past Warwick Grove where my mate Shackie used to live. His dad was still there. I saw his tiny frame in the window as I walked past but I doubt he would have remembered me. His mum and dad used to sit in separate rooms. He'd listen to Margaret Thatcher speeches on CD while she watched *Coronation Street*. Their bathroom window was still round. We'd go there for barbecues in summer and he handed out this cheap lager called Compass and one time Pete Booth puked on the stairs.

Walking down Manchester Road I saw the tram lines where the Metrolink came through. I carried on towards Droylsden past Aldwinians Rugby Club and then finally reached the Connie Club. I buzzed to be let in and Scoie wasn't in there. I gave him a bell and he said they'd decided to watch the match in the Lazy Toad instead.

There was a bouncer on the door and the pub was packed. They had the United game on in one side and the City game on in the other. I found Scoie and Shackie, who'd got there early and had a seat at a table right in front of the big screen showing the City game.

'Merry Christmas,' I said, brushing the rain off my coat.

'Ha, ha, here he is! Did you get yourself a pint?' said Shackie.

'No. Nearly though. I'll get them in anyway. What you on?'

'Two Carling, mate,' said Scoie.

The bar was rammed. Three barmaids rushed around serving. I recognised the older two. I came back with the pints and sat at the table. Scoie showed me his wedding ring and told me it was made of titanium. Shackie said it looked like a fucking washer. Then this bloke came and stood right in front of the big screen.

'Excuse me, mate,' shouted Scoie.

'What's up, our kid?' the man shouted back.

'Can't see, mate.'

'Any room on that fucking table then? You've been hogging it since about two bells.'

We all shoved round and this bloke sat down, putting his red can of Woodpecker on the table.

'On the cider, eh?' said Shackie.

'Sharp you, aren't you? Fighting juice. This is my own an' all.'

'Cheeky fucker.'

'Who are you calling a cheeky fucker?'

'They don't even serve that in here, do they? You'd get a fine for that in the Connie Club.'

'What's up lad, bad Christmas?'

'No, good one actually.'

'Ask him about his free turkey,' said Scoie.

'Fuck off, Scoie,' said Shackie.

'He could have got a twenty-five quid turkey for nowt but his mate only told him this morning!'

'Ha ha ha. Come on, lad. Cheer the fuck up. It is Christmas.'

'Alright, granddad, just drink your Woodpecker, you tight bastard.'

The game started and City missed a load of chances and it was obvious they'd pay for it later in the game. On the plus side United were losing. The old bloke shouted across to the other side of the bar, 'United are shit, United are shit!'

The old bloke continued to bait the reds on the other side of the bar, even when it wasn't looking good for City. And he kept baiting Shackie too. He kept trying it with me but I just laughed. I told him he'd be alright once he came out of his shell. When he said I was a bit quiet I replied that he never stopped for air and so I couldn't get a word in edgeways.

'Fucking hell, you need ear plugs with him, don't you?' said Shackie to the bloke's wife, who'd just come in.

'She wants a long-service medal that woman,' I said, sharing a smile with her. He laughed and smiled and began talking to her quietly. It seemed like she'd also had a few. The bloke stopped baiting the reds in the other side of the bar, and he also stopped baiting us. When we left I shook the old bloke's hand and smiled at his wife and wished them a Merry Christmas.

Most people in Droylsden are okay. The union jack flags are nothing to be scared about. You can't be up your own arse or too enthusiastic, that's the main thing. If someone asks you about yourself then keep it brief or else all you'll get is, 'I don't want your fucking life story'.

I remembered one of the barmaids in the Lazy Toad as I made the long walk home down Ashton Old Road. We'd gone back to hers and done it on her parents' bed because they were away for the weekend. We met a week later in the White Hart and had absolutely nothing to say to each other. That pub has gone now. I saw her a year or so later with a gangly lad in glasses. She looked so tired, pushing her pram through the puddles.

I carried on up Ashton Old Road. Openshaw looked to be changing but it was just the same. New budget supermarkets and takeaways and cheap-looking housing built for immigrants had replaced previous versions of the same thing. I wandered on past Smithfield Market. On Sunday mornings that place was packed with people of all nationalities coming to buy cheap fruit and veg. A fox ran across Grey Mare Lane. I carried on past a massive scrap metal yard piled with rubble. There was a car showroom, and an Enterprise car rental place where a pub had once been. I passed Pin Mill Brow and followed the path beside the Mancunian Way, under railway arches with abandoned cars and beer cans and oily puddles and the smell of piss. There were the five-a-side pitches at the Powerleague place in Ardwick. I'd tried a game of five-a-side a few months before but my knee had packed up again. I still wanted to take a ball onto there and kick it around. I walked over and stared at the moonlit pitches. I punched the metal fence and bruised my knuckles. Then I cut through down the back of Ardwick Green Park, not far from the Apollo. There was a butty shop that I remembered from my time working in the warehouse. I went past the Territorial Army place then skirted the dodgy estate that ran from Brunswick Street to Kincardine Road. I turned down Grosvenor Street, past the abandoned glass-strewn playground near Claire Street and a knitwear factory with barbed wire over its gates. There were Asian men sleeping in taxis. I looked up at the bright lights of all the high-rise flats: Lamport Court, Lockton Court, Silkin Court. I cut through past Litcham Close onto Lamport Close, and in the car park of the flats there was Riggers. He was sitting in a car with the door open. I kept walking, hoping he wouldn't notice me. At the door to the flats I reached into my pocket for the entry fob. He shouted over, 'Hey wanker!' I ignored it but he shouted again. 'Hey! Leave the door open!' If he lived there then he should have had a fob. It pissed me off. I shut the door behind me. He ran over and banged on it. He smiled at me and then ran a finger across his throat.

I nicked a shedload of books from the library. Sunday was the perfect opportunity. Most of them had never been out on loan and I felt I was putting them to use. I stuffed them down my pants just before it was time to go home, and halfway down Chapel Street I'd fish them out. But they had the reference number on the spine, and it was laminated over. They just didn't look as good on my bookshelf as all the others. I kept *Carnegie Hall with Tin Walls* but took the others back one at a time.

On the second floor, near the maps, was the journals section. On a Monday I went up there with just a handful of new journals and didn't come back downstairs for hours. I looked through all the magazines, and found a copy of *Ambit*, edited by Martin Bax. There was an early story by JG Ballard in there. And the library subscribed to a poetry magazine, PN *Review*, based in Manchester, and I read through a copy, particularly enjoying the cantankerous editorial. I sat with these journals at a table in front of a big window. There was a view stretching out across to the wind farms that desecrate the Lancashire hills. I could also see the big ventilation tower of Strangeways prison over to the right, but the tower of the Boddington's Brewery had long since been demolished to make way for a car park. The sun shone in through the window and I drifted in and out of sleep as a handful of students worked quietly around me.

After waking up I wandered down to the staff room where people were eating sandwiches and picking bits of fruit out of plastic containers with plastic forks. They'd been dealing with student enquiries all morning and none of them had any desire to talk. There was a woman there who had a tattoo of a Dewey Decimal number between her shoulder blades. I asked her about it and she looked like she wanted to kill herself. She said it was the number for *The Lord of the Rings*. There were wooden shutters across the windows, cutting out most of the natural light. A notice pinned on the fridge door read: *Whoever is eating my yoghurts please stop it.*

I'd managed to avoid Riggers so far. I was sure the whistling carried on but I slept through it. I began to think that he had gone again, but as I walked out of my front door one afternoon he was leaning on the walkway rail, looking across at the Etihad. He was wearing a City shirt. He rubbed his bald head and stroked his goatee beard. I walked straight past him and he said, 'Matter of time, sunbeam, matter of time.'

I thought of dragging him out of view of the cameras and fighting him, but whatever I did that wouldn't be the end of it. Scrotes like that don't quit. Weeks at a time passed without me seeing him, but when I did he always made that sign across his throat. If I saw his girlfriend she always started shouting at me and I was getting sick of it.

When I came home from the pub one night he was waiting by my door.

'Fancy another beer?' he said.

'Why not?' I said. I was pissed and I didn't care any more. Something had to give.

A bare bulb dangled from the ceiling. All the windows were covered with black sheets even though it was dark outside. I went for a slash and the bathroom was full of cannabis plants. The water in the bog was black. It flushed on the third try.

I washed my hands. There was a grey cake of soap, and hair clogging the sink.

I walked into the living room and he passed me a can of lager from a batch on the floor. They had come from a cash and carry. I looked over at the door leading through to the bedroom. There was a throwing star stuck in the back of it and the wood was peppered with holes.

'You've got some balls coming in here,' he said, stroking his goatee.

'I'm just drinking your beer, chief.'

'Chief? What the fuck is that?'

I gulped it down. We sat in silence, staring at each other. I went to get myself another beer. He put his hand on my forearm and squeezed it tightly. 'I'll decide who is having the beer.'

'Where's the hooker?' I asked. His eyes blazed. He'd been trying to play it cool. I didn't give a fuck.

'If you call her a hooker one more time you'll get a fucking knife in your stomach.'

'Go for it. She's a prostitute. End of story.'

'I said shut your fucking mouth!'

'You know Jake? Black guy on my floor? He told me. A fiver, he said.'

'He told *me* that you played for City. That's bollocks.'

'He's right. Was on the under-18s. Platt Lane. Are you going to stop whistling now?'

'Fuck off.'

'Don't spit the dummy.'

'Fuck off.'

'Do you love her?'

'Course I fucking love her.'

'Well, sorry to piss on your chips, chief. Maybe she doesn't do it any more. I never went with her if that makes any difference.'

'My dad played for City,' he said, quietly, while looking at the lino floor.

'Up the blues,' I said, then got up and walked out of there, never to see him again.

It is the start of a new year. I sit in the Crescent with Dom. He goes home after a couple of slowly sipped pints. I start to walk back, via pubs. First stop is the King's Arms, and I sit with an old boozer with a New Zealand accent and a wide-brimmed hat above a long, bulbous, veiny boozer's conk of a nose. He tells me all about Rousseau and Diderot. There are some actors sitting nearby, talking about the play they are rehearsing in the room upstairs. I recognise one from a bit part on TV. He looks pleased that I recognise him.

Leaving the King's Arms I go past the characterless Salford Central, tempted to smash the glass frontage beneath the CCTV. I pass the Mark Addy and look down at the moonlit Irwell, thinking of Henry Miller's descriptions of the Seine. I duck into Mulligan's just off Bridge Street. Being a Monday night it is virtually empty. Just a man reading a *Manchester Evening News*. I quibble at the price of the Guinness and he tells me that it's the best Guinness in town. I sip a Bushmill's and leave.

A streetlight wobbles in the wind. Crossing the road I walk down the chevrons in the middle for a few yards. One car waits at the traffic lights but otherwise the streets are silent. I look into the sky for peregrines.

Next on the route home is the Temple of Convenience. On the way in I see a sign in the window that reads 'No football shirts'. I sit near the toilet to save time. From my seat I can't help seeing the clock on the wall. I rub my beard and listen to Elbow. The Temple starts to fill up. I catch glances from both the barman and a group of musicians that make me feel uncomfortable. I have another piss and leave.

I go to O'Shea's, where they make no boasts about the Guinness. I walk the short route to the Lass O'Gowrie, where it seems that they welcome the solitary drinker, are used to it at least, maybe depend on it. I sit down without really looking where I'm sitting, near another solitary drinker, and he mutters to himself and moves to another seat.

I think about where to go next. I get to the Sandbar and remember why I prefer pubs to bars. The barmaid is there but her breasts aren't how I remember them. A diet has reduced their majesty. I have another drink. I have been drinking so much that I cannot get drunk. I try a Jameson's. I drink it fast so that it burns my mouth. There is a Greek bloke standing at the bar. He is friendly enough. I realise that he has been standing there for years. He smiles the same way as always. His hair is grey and his face is wrinkled. I act like I don't want to talk to anybody, but the barmaid and the Greek know the act.

The injury at City was years ago. Denise had gone for ever. It was time to get a grip. I had been close to turning things around when I'd given up drinking before and now I would do it again. Writing didn't make me happy and I knew it never would. But it was all I had left. I thought back to when I'd felt happiest without Denise: walking in the countryside. I thought about moving. You could rent a house for about five hundred a month on the Isle of Arran and I had happy memories of there. But I couldn't even afford the train fare to the Lakes.

I had a walk in Cheshire instead. I got off the train at Alderley Edge and headed up the road towards the cricket ground. I looked at the ground for a while and thought maybe I could have been a cricketer. There were old people playing on the tennis courts. From there I took the footpath up through a forest and emerged onto the edge, a rocky escarpment with a view stretching across to the Peak District hills. The sky was blue. I watched buzzards until they flew away. Getting up I took one of the many paths. The edge is the wooded hillside you can see from the train on the way to Crewe. I headed down to Edge House Farm and cut through Alder Wood and watched a heron in the trees high above a lake near Hare Hill. I walked down the road for a while and then took another footpath. I could see the Jodrell Bank observatory through the haze. I passed through picture-postcard scenery, little houses made up of distinctive bright brick with tidy lawns and immaculate picket fences. I walked down an old cobbled road between tall trees, thought of horses and carts rattling through there. There were glossy horses in the surrounding fields, a buzzard sitting on a wall, a heron by a mere. There were woods and farms and mills. Jays in the trees. Bird boxes and feeders. I walked slowly and kept stopping to look around. There was no traffic noise whatsoever. I wallowed in the birdsong. There was a kestrel on a telegraph wire. A man painted his window frames, a woman tended her flowers. When I looked over at them they smiled and said hello. I followed the cobbled lanes back to Alderley.

The calm started to fade as I walked through the town centre. But the train was quiet, and I held on to some of my serenity until a load of people got on at Hazel Grove, and then a load more at Stockport and Heaton Chapel. The faces weren't like the ones I'd seen in the countryside. Eyes were focused on tablets and phones and nobody seemed to look through the window.

I had to get out of Lamport Court. I didn't want to get involved with someone like Riggers. I started looking on Rightmove. I would have liked to have moved to a little house in the countryside but around Alderley Edge the money was ridiculous. Alderley Edge is where the footballers live. I looked at the Peak District, and though the rents seemed reasonable it would cost me a fortune to get into work from there.

I finally found a place I could afford and I moved out. After putting the last of my stuff in the hired van I went back up to the flat and locked up. With my finger I wrote '£5' in the dust on the windowsill and I wish I hadn't.

It was a tiny bedsit and the rent cost a little more. But Didsbury was affluent and I wouldn't have to look over my shoulder every time I walked down the street. There were no pimps and hookers and druggies in the building. The bottle bank got a hammering from wine bottles, and there could be a crowd at the Cheese Hamlet, but that was about it. The windows were single glazed and cold air circulated in the cellar beneath my feet. It was freezing in there. I folded out a tiny futon and woke every morning with a stiff neck. But the room got the sun in the morning and I couldn't hear any traffic. There was a palm tree in the garden and when its shadow fell on my wall I thought of Los Angeles. I cycled to work down Barlow Moor Road and through Whalley Range. City were winning trophies and I started my second book.

There was a second-hand bookshop around the corner, run by an old bloke called Bob. He cycled there and locked his bike against a lamppost outside. He had a lot of books and there was barely room to move. I saw my first book. I took it down off the shelf and opened it. Inside there was the dedication, *To Denise, with all my love.*

Acknowledgements

THANKS TO NICHOLAS Royle, as tenacious an editor as he is a full back. Thanks to my Dad for taking me to Maine Road all those years. Thanks to John G Hall, a fine poet and once on the books at City. Thanks to Scoie, for the friendship, the subs and the spare tickets. Thanks to Sergio Agüero for *that* goal. Thanks to Paul Lake, who had everything as a footballer, and whose autobiography *I'm Not Really Here* provided inspiration for this novel. Thanks to Bruce Springsteen for his music. And thanks once again to Chris and Jen at Salt.

NEW FICTION FROM SALT

KERRY HADLEY-PRYCE
The Black Country (978-1-78463-034-8)

CHRISTINA JAMES
The Crossing (978-1-78463-041-6)

IAN PARKINSON
The Beginning of the End (978-1-78463-026-3)

CHRISTOPHER PRENDERGAST
Septembers (978-1-907773-78-5)

MATTHEW PRITCHARD
Broken Arrow (978-1-78463-040-9)

JONATHAN TAYLOR
Melissa (978-1-78463-035-5)

GUY WARE
The Fat of Fed Beasts (978-1-78463-024-9)

This book has been typeset by
SALT PUBLISHING LIMITED
using Neacademia, a font designed by Sergei Egorov
for the Rosetta Type Foundry in the Czech Republic.
It is manufactured using Creamy 70gsm, a Forest
Stewardship Council™ certified paper from Stora Enso's
Anjala Mill in Finland. It was printed and bound by
Clays Limited in Bungay, Suffolk, Great Britain.

CROMER, NORFOLK
GREAT BRITAIN
MMXVI